A Wolf at the Door

A Wolf at the Door

and Other Retold Fairy Tales

Edited by

Ellen Datlow and

Terri Windling

Aladdin Paperbacks

New York London Toronto Sydney Singapore

This book is dedicated to Jane Yolen, who has been
a good friend to the old fairy tales . . . and to us
Ellen Datlow and Terri Windling

First Aladdin Paperbacks edition December 2001

Introduction copyright © 2000 by Terri Windling ✦ "The Months of Manhattan" copyright ©
2000 by Delia Sherman ✦ "Cinder Elephant" copyright © 2000 by Jane Yolen ✦ "Instructions"
copyright © 2000 by Neil Gaiman ✦ "Mrs. Big" copyright © 2000 by Michael Cadnum ✦
"Falada" copyright © 2000 by Nancy Farmer ✦ "A Wolf at the Door" copyright © 2000 by
Tanith Lee ✦ "Ali Baba and the Forty Aliens" copyright © 2000 by Janeen Webb ✦ "Swans"
copyright © 2000 by Kelly Link ✦ "The Kingdom of Melting Glances" copyright © 2000 by
Katherine Vaz ✦ "Hansel's Eyes" copyright © 2000 by Garth Nix ✦ "Becoming Charise" copy-
right © 2000 by Kathe Koja ✦ "The Seven Stage a Comeback" copyright © 2000 by Gregory
Maguire ✦ "The Twelve Dancing Princesses" copyright © 2000 by Patricia A. McKillip

Aladdin Paperbacks
An imprint of Simon & Schuster
Children's Publishing Division
1230 Avenue of the Americas
New York, NY 10020

All rights reserved, including the right of
reproduction in whole or in part in any form.
Also available in a Simon & Schuster Books for Young Readers hardcover edition.
Designed by Steve Scott
The text of this book was set in Adobe Caslon.
Printed and bound in the United States of America
10 9 8 7 6 5 4 3 2 1

The Library of Congress has cataloged the hardcover edition as follows:
A wolf at the door : and other retold fairy tales / edited by Ellen Datlow and Terri Windling.
p. cm.
Contents: The Months of Manhattan / Delia Sherman — Cinder elephant / Jane Yolen —
Instructions / Neil Gaiman — Mrs. Big / Michael Cadnum — Falada / Nancy Farmer — A
Wolf at the door / Tanith Lee — Ali Baba and the forty aliens / Janeen Webb — Swans / Kelly
Link — The Kingdom of Melting Glances / Katherine Vaz — Hansel's eyes / Garth Nix —
Becoming Charise / Kathe Koja — The Seven stage a comeback / Gregory Maguire —
The twelve dancing princesses / Patricia A. McKillip.
ISBN 0-689-82138-7 (hc.)
1. Fairy tales. [1. Fairy tales.]
I. Datlow, Ellen. II. Windling, Terri.
PZ8.W813   2000
[Fic]—dc21   99-38616
CIP
ISBN 1-4169-0813-7 (Aladdin pbk.)

Contents

Introduction
by Terri Windling and Ellen Datlow

The stories in this book are based on classic fairy tales—but probably not the way you've ever heard fairy tales before. Most people think that fairy tales are stories meant for very young children, but hundreds of years ago tales of magic were loved by folks of all ages. The fairy tales we all know today—like "Cinderella," "Hansel and Gretel," "Snow White," and all the rest—used to be darker, stranger, and more complex, until this century. Then they were turned into children's tales, banished to the nursery (as J. R. R. Tolkien, the author of *The Lord of the Rings* once pointed out) like furniture adults have grown tired of and no longer want. The stories were changed and simplified when they were rewritten for very young readers. And it's these sweet and simple versions that most of us know today.

But if you go back to the older versions, you'll see why people both old and young liked to gather before the hearth fire and listen to these marvelous stories on long, cold winter evenings. Fairy tales were scarier then, and the heroes and heroines were more interesting. Cinderella, for instance, was a smart, feisty, angry girl in the oldest versions of the story (dating back all the way to ninth-century China), not the helpless dreamer who has to be saved by a prince, as we know her today. Happy endings were not guaranteed. Red Riding Hood was gobbled up by the wolf, Rapunzel's lover was blinded by the witch, and the Little Mermaid died when her fickle prince took a human wife. The old fairy tales, like all the best stories, were filled with all the dark and bright, all the failures and triumphs, that life has to offer. No wonder our ancestors have loved them for hundreds and hundreds of years.

All of the writers in this book loved fairy tales when they were young, and they didn't stop loving and reading them even when they grew to adulthood. Each writer has taken a favorite tale and made a brand-new story from it—stories full of strangeness, humor, dark magic, and wonder.

These are tales to lead you into the Dark Woods, where witches live and animals talk and magic appears when you least expect it. And here are a few standard words of advice when you enter that enchanted forest: Be kind to old women on the path (they may be fairies in disguise). Use magic wishes carefully (you'll get exactly what you wish for). Don't eat the food the fairies offer (it will trap you in their realm forever). And be sure to leave a trail of stones to find your way home again. . . .

The Months of Manhattan

by Delia Sherman

Liz Wallach was a pretty good kid. She mostly did her homework on time and pretty much got along with her father and was usually polite to her girlfriends. She wasn't perfect, by any means. She had been known to lie about brushing her teeth and she couldn't for the life of her tell her left from her right. But for a ten-year-old, she wasn't bad.

Liz lived with her father in a big apartment on the Upper West Side of New York City. Sometimes she went to stay with her mother in San Francisco or her grandmother on Cape Cod. She liked school. Things were good.

Then Beth Dodson came into her life.

Beth Dodson was the daughter of one of Dad's girlfriends. When the girlfriend became Liz's stepmother, Liz and Beth became stepsisters. Liz was ready to be happy about this. She'd always wanted a sister, and she

1

kind of liked it that their real names were the same: Elizabeth.

But Beth had been perfectly happy being an only child, and she didn't like it at all that they had the same name. That was only one of the things she didn't like. She didn't like school and she didn't like Chinese food and she didn't like New York. It was big and noisy and dirty, and there were too many people living in it.

"Maybe she's shy," said Liz's father hopefully. "Maybe she'll get over it."

But Beth had no intention of getting over hating New York, or anything else. She whined constantly: about having to walk three blocks to the bus stop, about having ballet lessons at Mme. Demipointe's École de Danse.

She fought with her mother, and wouldn't speak to Liz or her stepfather except to say that she wished she were still living in New Rochelle with her daddy and playing soccer on Wednesday afternoons.

Things weren't so good anymore.

It was November, just before Thanksgiving vacation, when Liz got a special history assignment. She had to go to the American Wing at the Metropolitan Museum of Art and look at the furniture and write a paper about it.

Liz's stepmother said, "I can take you while Bethy's in ballet class. You'll have to be quick, though. Mme. Demipointe hates to be kept waiting."

Delia Sherman

By the time Liz and her stepmother dropped Beth off at Mme. Demipointe's and got to the museum, it was about 3:00 P.M. Liz's stepmother paid for two admissions, went to the restaurant, sat down at a little round table, and took a magazine out of her bag.

"Aren't you coming with me?" Liz asked.

"It's your assignment," said her stepmother. "It's better if you do it yourself. And remember, we have to be at Madame's by four-thirty."

"But I don't know where—"

"I don't either," said her stepmother. "Ask."

By the time Liz found a guard who wasn't busy with someone else, ten minutes of her hour were gone. Then she turned left instead of right in the Medieval Treasury and got lost, and asked another guard and got lost again. Precious minutes ticked away as she walked through rooms of paintings and statues.

Finally, at 3:45, she walked up a flight of stairs and through a glass door, and found herself in a small, dark room with nothing in it but a big, bright picture.

Wherever she was, it wasn't the American Wing.

Liz wasn't much of a crier as a general rule, but this was too much. Even if she started back now and didn't get lost once, she'd be late, and her stepmother would be madder than a taxi driver in a traffic jam and her assignment still wouldn't be done. "I must be just about the unluckiest person in the world," she wailed.

"Whatsa matter, kid?"

The voice was friendly, with a heavy Bronx accent. Liz wiped her face on her sleeve and looked around for a guard, but she was alone.

The painting caught her eye.

It showed the statue of Atlas at Rockefeller Center with twelve people standing and sitting around it. They were all ages, from a very little girl in a snowsuit with cat ears to an old man in a wheelchair, and all the races Liz had ever heard of, except maybe Native American. They were wearing all kinds of different clothes, too, from a little Hispanic boy in snow boots and a ski jacket to a young, white guy in Bermuda shorts. A pretty African-American woman in a sundress opened her painted lips and said, "What is it, honey? Maybe we can help."

Liz's heart started to beat very fast. She was startled, but not frightened. She'd read lots of books in which things like this happened. "I'm lost," she said.

"We also," said a Pakistani boy in baggy jeans and a hooded sweatshirt. "But you have found us."

Liz thought about this. "Would you like me to tell the guard you're here?"

The old man in the wheelchair laughed. He was pale and thin as a china cup, but his laugh was warm and strong. "No. Thank you. We prefer to be found by chance."

"Oh," Liz said, and glanced at her watch: 3:40. She'd thought it was later.

"What time of year is it?" The question came from

Delia Sherman

an Asian girl about Liz's age, dressed in a red slicker and boots and flowered mittens.

"November," said Liz.

"I hate November," the girl said, and stuck out her tongue at an old African-American woman leaning on a cane.

"It's not so bad," said Liz. "There's Thanksgiving and hot apple cider, and we get to go to Grandma's. And then it's almost December, and that means Christmas and I can go sledding in Central Park with Dad." She remembered Beth and sighed. "If he still wants to."

"January, though," remarked a middle-aged Latino man in an embroidered short-sleeved shirt. "January is very terrible."

"And February, and March," added a skinny, unshaven man dressed in layers and layers of brown jackets.

"I kind of like February and March," Liz said. "I like getting cold and wet and then coming in and getting warm and looking at the lights out the window. It's easier to go to school in winter, too. You don't want to be outdoors so much, unless it's snowing, of course."

"Of course," said a woman with a prayer shawl around her shoulders. "But April, you know what they say about April, no? April is the cruelest month, that's what they say."

"April showers bring May flowers," said Liz. "Besides, I like mud and the way it smells."

"Even in Central Park?" asked an old Hispanic woman with a cane.

"Especially in Central Park."

"And the summer?" asked a teenage girl with her hair in a million little braids and flowers painted on her nails.

"Oh, summer is neat," said Liz. "May and June can be hard because I want to be outside all the time and there's still school, but it smells so good and the days are getting longer and there's summer vacation coming and we go to Cape Cod, and that's the best."

"So you must hate the fall," said a little African-American boy in a very big parka.

"Not really," said Liz. "I miss my friends over the summer, and there's my birthday in October, and I love the leaves turning all red and gold and—" she stopped suddenly. "Listen. This is way cool, but I'm really late, and my stepmother is going to kill me. I really have to go."

"I think we can take care of that for you," said the young guy in shorts. "Can't we, September?"

The woman smoothed her prayer shawl. "I think we should, June. And the history assignment as well." She caught sight of Liz's face and laughed kindly. "We can't do it for you—that wouldn't be kosher. But we can give you the time to do it in. And directions to the American Wing."

"Bye-bye," said the little girl in the snowsuit. "Good luck."

And they were gone.

Oh, there was still a painting on the wall, but it was just a big canvas with bright blobs on it that only looked like people if you stood back and squinted hard. The plaque on the wall beside it read: THE TWELVE MONTHS OF MANHATTAN. PETER MINUIT. UNDATED.

Liz looked at her watch. It was 3:05 P.M. She had fifty-five minutes before her stepmother would be looking for her. She ran straight to the American Wing without taking one wrong turn, and looked at the furniture and took notes for her paper until her watch said 3:50, when she walked back to the restaurant without even having to ask for directions. It was magical.

As Liz came up to her stepmother's table, she looked at her watch. "Four o'clock exactly," she said, surprised. "Lucky for you you made it."

Outside, it was raining, a cold, thick November rain. There wasn't a taxi to be seen, and lots of people were waiting.

"We're going to be hours late picking Beth up," Liz's stepmother moaned.

Just then, a taxi pulled up right in front of Liz. The door opened, the passenger got out, and Liz's stepmother nipped right in, with Liz on her heels. Liz's stepmother told the taxi where they were going, and sat back as the traffic miraculously cleared to let them through. "What a piece of luck!" she exclaimed.

Liz hung on to her notebook and grinned.

From that moment on, things got much, much better.

Not only did taxis stop whenever Liz needed one, she always made it to the bus stop just when the bus was pulling up to it. Her dad gave her a sled for Christmas, and her stepmother liked the scarf Liz knitted for her. And she never, ever lost a card game. Old Maid, Go Fish, War—anything where luck counted, Liz just couldn't lose.

"Not again!" her stepmother groaned as Liz stripped her of her hoarded sixes and triumphantly laid down all her own cards.

"Look at the bright side, dear," said her father. "If we need money, we can just send her to buy a lottery ticket."

"I'm only ten," Liz objected. "They wouldn't sell me one."

Beth's mother glanced at Beth, who was looking as gloomy as the East River in the rain. "I'm tired of cards," she said.

"Monopoly!" Beth's stepfather said cheerfully, and got out the board. "I'll take the top hat. I never lose a game when I have the top hat."

He lost this game, though. Liz won it, mostly because she landed on Boardwalk, Park Place, and all the Railroads her first time around the board.

"Lucky stiff," her father said.

"Too lucky," Beth muttered, and went off to think about it. Ever since that trip to the museum in

Delia Sherman

November, Liz had been luckier than any human being had a right to be. Something had to have happened, something magic. It wasn't fair. Nice things were always happening to Liz, and only bad things happened to her.

Later, Beth challenged Liz to a game of Paper, Scissors, Stone. Unable to think of a reason not to, Liz agreed. Seven times, the stepsisters chanted, "One, Two Three, Go." Seven times, Liz won.

"That's not luck, that's magic," Beth said accusingly. "You have to tell me what happened. I want to be lucky, too."

Liz thought about lying, but it just didn't seem right. Beth wouldn't find the Months of Manhattan unless they wanted her to. And if she did find them, Liz was sure they'd be able to handle one eleven-year-old girl, even one as whiny and annoying as Beth.

So she told her stepsister all about getting really lost, and stumbling into a room with a magic picture in it. She would have told her all about the Seasons, but Beth didn't want to hear about it.

"I'm not a total idiot," she said. "If you tell me everything, it'll ruin the magic, right? I hate you, Liz Wallach."

Next day, Beth announced at dinner that her history teacher had given her the now-famous American Wing furniture assigment. It was due Monday.

"But the museum's a madhouse on weekends," her mother objected.

"We can make a family outing of it," said her stepfather. "It'll be fun."

Beth pouted. "I want to do it by myself."

Her stepfather said, "Good for you, Bethy. We'll turn you into a New Yorker yet. I tell you what. We'll all go to the museum, and you can go to the American Wing and the rest of us will look at armor or something and we'll all meet in the restaurant for lunch."

And that was what they did. Liz, her dad, and Beth's mother went off one way, and Beth went off in another. She'd never liked going to the museum, so it wasn't very long before she was as lost and frightened as the most demanding magic would wish. The museum was, as her mother had predicted, a madhouse. Everywhere she turned, people bumped into her and glared at her. Thinking of nothing but finding somewhere quiet, she ran up a back stairway and through a glass door and found herself in a small, dark room with nothing in it but a large, bright picture.

In her fear, Beth had almost forgotten what had brought her to the museum. Almost, but not quite. She stared at the picture to see if it looked magic. It didn't. What could be magic about a bunch of street people sitting around a stupid statue?

"It was a dumb idea, anyway," she said aloud. "Everyone knows there's no such thing as magic."

"Who says?"

Beth jumped. One of the people in the painting, a

Delia Sherman

dark brown boy about her age in huge, baggy jeans, was scowling at her.

Beth said, "Remember my stepsister, Liz? She was here in November. You made her lucky."

Next to a guy in bermuda shorts was an African-American girl with long nails and lots of braids. "November," she said. "I know November. Is it still winter, out there in the world?"

Beth shook her head scornfully. "You guys are supposed to be magic, right? And you don't even know what month it is? It's December, for your information, and it's cold and wet, and I hate it."

"What about Christmas, and the snow?" asked the young guy in shorts.

"It doesn't snow in New York, not a real snow like at home. It just turns into slush and puddles that get into your boots. And Christmas isn't the same without Daddy. I hate winter here, every bit of it."

"And spring?" asked an old bum wearing about a million raggedy jackets.

"It never gets warm until June, and then it gets hot and muggy, and you can smell the garbage and you never feel clean. And then it gets cold again, just like that, and starts raining again, and there aren't even any pretty leaves to look at, like there are at home. I hate it. I hate it all."

The Months exchanged silent looks.

"Well," said the woman in the prayer shawl. "We

certainly know where you stand." Her voice was angry, in a cool sort of way.

Beth scowled. "You *asked*," she whined. "That's how I feel. I can't help it if you don't like it. Now you'll probably do something awful to me. It's not fair."

"Don't you worry, honey," said an African-American woman in a sundress. "We're going to give you exactly what you need. And I don't want to hear any of your sass, April."

The baggy-jeans boy shrugged and grinned.

The old man in the wheelchair lifted a hand like a white claw and said, "The luck you have asked for is yours. Now go."

Beth felt a giant hand shove her out of the little room. It kept on shoving her, right and left through the Saturday crowds, until she was, if possible, even more lost than she had been before. And then it left her, in the farthest corner of European Decorative Arts, in a room full of cloudy glass cups.

By the time Beth had found her way back to the restaurant, she was nearly an hour late. Her mother and stepfather, who had been wondering if she'd been kidnapped, were pretty mad when she showed up safe and sound. When they found out that she didn't have any notes on American furniture, they were even madder. And when she unluckily let slip that she didn't really have a paper due Monday, they were mad enough to fight all the lions in the Bronx Zoo and win.

Delia Sherman

The only person who wasn't mad at Beth was Liz. At first, it was because she thought that having major bad luck served Beth right. But before long, she started to feel sorry for her. Anyone would.

Beth couldn't walk down the street without stepping in chewing gum or doggy doo. Streetlights turned red when she came to the corner, and buses pulled away just as she got to the stop. When it rained, her umbrella inevitably blew inside out, and taxis going too fast splashed her with dirty water. She caught every cold that was going around, and in April, she sprained her ankle in ballet class. In June, she came down with the measles.

At first, all the bad luck made Beth meaner than ever. She was especially mean to Liz, who she blamed for ruining her life.

"It's pretty awful," Liz agreed. "But I bet there's a way to break the curse—there usually is, in fairy tales. Maybe if you apologized to the Months. Or at least made it up to them somehow."

"Apologize?" growled Beth. "Why should I apologize? They're the ones who should apologize, for doing this to me. You're a creep." She made a grab at Liz's braid, missed, and fell out of bed onto Barbie's Dream House, scraping her arm painfully.

"Oh, poor Beth," said Liz. "But it wouldn't have happened if you hadn't tried to pull my hair. Think about it."

Beth was too miserable to answer her. But later, when the measles were itching like crazy and even her mother didn't want to keep her company, she thought about what Liz had said. What were the old man's words? "The luck you have asked for is yours." Maybe she had hurt the Months' feelings. Maybe there was something nice about June in New York she just hadn't noticed.

She looked out the window. The sky was clear, a deep turquoise blue that made the buildings across the street look bright and sharp. A pigeon landed on her windowsill with a flutter of gray wings and cooed at her.

Okay. Maybe June in New York wasn't so bad after all.

Once Beth had noticed the pigeon and the sky, she began to notice other things. She noticed that her mother kept bringing her food and books even when Beth threw them on the floor. She noticed that the rocks Liz brought her from Central Park had chips of mica in them that sparkled like tiny diamonds. She noticed that her stepfather always came into her room as soon as he got home from work and told her how they'd all go to Cape Cod in July and build sand castles together. She noticed that she kind of liked it when he did that.

By the time she was over her measles and everyone went to Cape Cod, she didn't hate New York City nearly as much as she had. What's more, she could find both her shoes when she needed them, and the tunnels under her sand castles didn't cave in, and the sand fleas bit everyone in the family, not just her.

It was like magic. By the time school started in the fall, Beth was down to little things that could happen to anyone, like losing pencils and leaving her gloves in taxis. She pretty much got along with Liz and was usually nice to her stepfather and mostly did her homework on time. She tried Chinese food and discovered that she liked it. In fact, Beth Dodson had become a pretty good kid.

That Thanksgiving, Beth and Liz decided to go back to the Metropolitan Museum to find the Twelve Months of Manhattan and thank them. But although the sisters did their best to get lost, they never found the back stairs that led to a small, dark room with nothing in it but a big, bright picture.

Delia Sherman's all-time favorite books are *The Merrie Adventures of Robin Hood* and *Fairy Tales from Many Lands*, which is where she first learned about the "Twelve Months" and the importance of being polite to people you don't know.

She is the author of two historical fantasy novels, *Through a Brazen Mirror* and *The Porcelain Dove*, and the forthcoming young adult time-travel novel *The Freedom Maze*. She is also coeditor of *The Essential Bordertown*, an "urban fantasy" anthology for teenage readers, and of *The Horns of Elfland*, a collection of stories about music and magic. She was born in Japan, grew up in New York City, and now lives in New York and Boston.

Cinder Elephant

by Jane Yolen

There was once a lovely big girl who lived with her father in a large house near the king's park.

Her mother had been called *Pleasingly Plump*. Her grandmother had been called *Round and Rosie*. Her great-grandmother had been called *Sunny and Solid*. And her great-great-grandmother had been called *Fat!*

But though she was bigger than most, the girl had a sweet face, a loving heart, a kind disposition, and big feet.

Her name was Eleanor.

Her father called her Elly.

Now Elly and her father did everything together. They rambled and scrambled over the rolling hills. They bird-watched and dish-washed and trout-fished and star-wished together.

In fact, they were happy for a long long time.

But one day Elly's father grew lonely for someone his own age; someone who laughed at the same jokes;

someone who knew the words to the same songs; someone who knew the steps to dances like the turkey trot and the mashed potato and didn't think those were just food groups.

So he married again, a woman so thin, it took her three tries to throw a shadow. She had two skinny daughters. One was as skinny as a straw. One was as skinny as a reed. They had thin smiles, too. And thin names: Reen and Rhee. And hearts so thin, you could read a magazine through them.

Reen and Rhee smiled their thin smiles all through the wedding and the very next morning they made Elly their maid.

They made her do the dishes. They made her make the beds. They even made her sit in the fireplace, where she got covered with soot and cinders.

To make matters worse, they called her names:

"Elly, Elly,
big fat belly,
Cinder Elephant."

So Elly cried.

But crying only made things worse. It made the soot into mud pies and the cinders into bogs. So Elly stopped crying.

Elly may have been big, but she wasn't stupid. She did the sisters' work without complaining, and she did it very well. And in her spare time—which meant long after her stepmother and the skinnies were asleep—she read books. Books about football and baseball, books about tennis and golf. It was how she preferred to get her exercise.

One day as Elly worked in the kitchen, two little bluebirds peeked in the window.

Elly guessed they were hungry, so she gave them each a crumb of bread.

Just then in came the skinnies, Reen and Rhee, one thin as a reed, one thin as a straw. "Mama, Mama," they screamed in their thin little voices. "Look what Cinder Elephant has done!"

Their skinny mother came quickly in her best running shoes, size five and a half, narrow. (Very narrow.)

She took the bread crumbs away, saying, "Cinder Elephant, this is all you will get for *your* dinner. Dieting will do you a world of good, and you will thank me for it later."

Then she turned to her skinny daughters. "I have great news. Prince Junior is home from school."

"The PRINCE!" Reen and Rhee squealed, for of course they had heard of him. He wore great clothes. He had straight teeth, which in the days before dentists took a lot of doing. And he was sure to inherit the kingdom.

The sisters smiled their thin smiles and ran to their

bedrooms to pick out their prettiest dresses to wear just in case they should bump into him.

Elly stayed on in the kitchen pretending to cry. But as soon as the skinnies were gone, she gave her bread crumb dinner to the bluebirds, anyway.

They ate it in one gulp each, singing:

> *"The bigger the heart,*
> *The greater the prize.*
> *You will be perfect*
> *In somebody's eyes."*

Fairy-tale birds always sing like this. It's annoying to everyone except the heroine.

Meanwhile in the palace, Prince Junior had just had a serious talk with his father, the king.

"Time to get married," said the king. "Time to grow up. Time to run the kingdom." The king always spoke that way to his son: short and to the point. Pointed remarks were his specialty.

"I am not in love," said Prince Junior.

"Doesn't matter," said the king.

"I am not even in like," said Prince Junior.

"Doesn't matter," said the king.

"I don't even know any girls," said Prince Junior.

"*That* matters," said the king. "Time to think about it." So, the king began to think.

Jane Yolen

It took hours.

It took days.

It took help!

At last the king came up with a plan. "Time for a ball," said the king.

Prince Junior was pleased. "Oh, good," he said. "I like balls." He meant he liked footballs and baseballs and tennis balls. (Though he wasn't terribly fond of moth-balls. They stank something fierce.)

"Your father means a fancy-dress, drinking-champagne-from-slippers ball," said his mother, the queen.

Prince Junior groaned. He really preferred watching birds to that kind of ball.

"Invite everyone in the kingdom," said the king, "as long as they are girls. Send them to every shop girl, cop girl, mop girl, prop girl, and champagne-in-the-slipper girl in the kingdom."

"And," added the queen, "no invitation—no admit-tance."

So invitations went out on creamy invitation paper, and every girl in the kingdom was invited except for Elly beecause her skinny stepsisters tore up her invita-tion. Then they made Elly pick up the creamy pieces.

On the night of the royal ball the skinny stepsisters swept out of the house, in yellow gowns, skinny as straws and looking like brooms. They rode to the castle, and their skinny mother went with them. And to the castle as well went every shop girl, cop girl, mop girl, prop girl, and champagne-in-the-slipper girl in the kingdom.

But Elly stayed at home staring into the cinders. She had no invitation to the ball. Even worse—she had nothing to wear.

At ten o'clock there came a noise at the kitchen window. It was the bluebirds.

> *"You gave us something*
> *Yummy to eat.*
> *Now we are back*
> *With a marvelous treat."*

Elly threw open the window.

In flew the bluebirds with all their bird friends carrying a large gown made of feathers. Blue feathers from the bluebirds, gold feathers from the goldfinches, green feathers from the greenfinches, and brown feathers from the owls.

They slipped the gown over Elly's head before she could say a word.

> *"You look beautiful," sang the bluebirds.*
> *"As trees in the fall*
> *And now you can set off*
> *For Prince Junior's ball."*

Jane Yolen

Actually, with all those feathers, Elly looked more like a big fat hen.

And as much as she wanted to go to the royal dance, Elly knew a thing or two about balls herself. She knew she could not get in without a proper invitation. But she did not want to hurt the birds' feelings.

So instead she said, "I have no dancing slippers. Size nine and a half, wide." (Very wide.)

The birds flew away all atwitter and did not return until eleven o'clock when they pecked excitedly at the kitchen window.

> "Let us in, let us in,
> We've come with a treat:
> A pair of new shoes
> To put on your feet."

(Please remember that the expression "birdbrain" was invented by someone who knew quite a bit about birds.)

Elly opened the window, and in flew the bluebirds with all their bird friends, carrying two big slippers made of twigs and grass, which they slipped on to Elly's feet.

"How do I look?" Elly asked.

Actually she looked like a big fat hen sitting on a nest. But the birds all thought she looked beautiful and said so.

Elly did not want to hurt their feelings. But she still had no invitation. So instead she said, "I have no carriage to ride in. And if I walk to the palace, I will be too late for the ball."

> *"Here we are*
> *Birds of a feather*
> *And so we all*
> *Must flock together,"*

the birds sang.

And before Elly could ask them what they meant, they had lifted her up and up and up.

The wind blew under the arms of the feather gown. And away Elly flew with the flock of birds to Prince Junior's fancy-dress ball.

By now, of course, it was nearly midnight.

Prince Junior was tired of talking about things he did not enjoy, like the weather and the price of fancy dresses. He was slightly sick from all that shoe champagne. So he went outside to the terrace for a breath of fresh air and to do a little bird watching.

He had just put his field glasses up to his eyes, when what should drop from the skies but a giant hen on a nest.

Prince Junior was amazed. He stared at the hen's lovely round face through his glasses. He checked his field guide.

There was no such hen among the chickens.

It was Elly, of course, come to the royal ball even though she had no invitation.

"Sorry to make an end run around the guards at the door," said Elly.

"You know football!" said the prince.

"And baseball," said Elly.

"What about tennis?" asked the prince.

"Adore it," she admitted. "Golf, too."

Prince Junior was not so sure about golf. So he asked slyly: "And mothballs?"

"Stink something fierce," said Elly.

"I think I love you," said the prince, smiling at Elly with his perfect teeth.

Just then a big wind blew across the terrace, lifting Elly in her feather dress back into the air.

One of her slippers fell off, landing in the undergrowth.

Then she was gone, blown back home before answering Prince Junior's declaration of love.

By the time she was dropped onto her own front porch, the feather gown was a ruin. She put the remaining slipper on the windowsill over the kitchen sink and filled it with ferns.

Poor Elly.

Poor prince.

The skinny sisters came home in a twit. That is not a kind of carriage. It is a kind of temper tantrum. They were so mad, they could barely talk. So they yelled.

"PRINCE JUNIOR IS A LOON," yelled Reen.

"WHICH IS A KIND OF BIRD," yelled Rhee.

"HE IS IN LOVE WITH A FAT HEN," they yelled together.

Elly just smiled into the cinders. It was a happy smile and a sad smile, too. But she didn't tell them anything. Would you?

Prince Junior found the slipper the very next day, when he was out bird watching, which some people do to ease an aching heart. He thought the slipper was a nest and he went to put it back in the tree.

But then he took a second look. "I know what this is!" he said. (He was pretty smart for a prince.) And he picked up the slipper and ran inside.

"I want to marry the hen who fits this grass slipper," he told his parents.

"Glass slippers are more usual," said his mother.

"Princes marry swans—not hens," added his father.

Then they sighed.

But Prince Junior was adamant.

So he searched high. (Very high.)

He searched low. (Very low.)

In fact, he searched the entire kingdom. But all the girls had small feet, tiny feet, five-to-seven, narrow feet. (Very narrow.) The grass slipper fell off every one.

Jane Yolen

At last Prince Junior arrived at Elly's house, the very last house on the very last block, where Elly sat amongst the cinders.

The skinny sisters tried on the grass shoe. They wadded paper in at the toes and cotton at the heel. They put Super Glue on their insteps and duct tape on their ankles.

But, still, the shoe fell off. (It was, after all, a slipper, which is to say, it was slippery.)

And then it fell apart all over the kitchen floor. (It was, after all, only made of grass and twigs.)

"Oh, no!" cried Prince Junior. "Now how will I find my own true love?"

The skinny sisters were furious. "Elly! Come clean up this mess," they demanded.

Then they swept out of the room with Prince Junior while Elly swept up the room by herself.

When she was done, Elly got the other slipper, from the windowsill. She was about to put it on her big foot to show Prince Junior who she really was, when she noticed that the bluebirds had used the slipper as a nest. There were three little eggs hidden in the ferns. So she put the slipper back on the sill, and sat down again in the cinders.

Poor Elly.

Poor Prince.

And that would have been the end of that, except the bluebirds came back to the nest and began to squawk and talk in bluebird.

Prince Junior heard their cries. He ran into the kitchen with his field glasses. "Bluebirds!" he cried.

"*Sialia sialis*," said Elly, which is the scientific name that only bird watchers seem to know or to care about.

Prince Junior turned his glasses from the nest to Elly. Close up, he recognized her face. "My dear hen!" he cried.

"My dear prince!" she answered.

Then they kissed, and all that nonsense about slippers—glass, grass, or good sturdy leather—was forgotten.

Elly and Prince Junior were married, of course. They named their children Blue, Green, Goldie, and Owl.

As for Reen and Rhee, and their skinny mother, they were often invited to the palace because Elly held no grudges. But they never came. Their lips were too thin to ask forgiveness, and their minds too mean to understand love.

Moral: If you love a waist, you waste a love.

Jane Yolen

Jane Yolen, who has more than two hundred books to her credit, including the Caldecott-winning *Owl Moon*, has always loved fairy tales. In fact, growing up, she read all of the Andrew Lang Color Fairy Books, which included folktales from around the world. She says: "'Cinder Elephant' has more to do with the fact that I wear a size nine and a half shoe and went from rompers to a size twelve dress with no intervening steps than any deep love for Cinderella. I hated the Disney *Cinderella* with a passion. All those mice. All those birds. The birds in 'Cinder Elephant' are a satire on those twittery bluebirds."

Instructions

Neil Gaiman

Touch the wooden gate in the wall you never
    saw before.
Say "please" before you open the latch,
go through,
walk down the path.
A red metal imp hangs from the green-painted
    front door,
as a knocker,
do not touch it; it will bite your fingers.
Walk through the house. Take nothing. Eat
    nothing.
However,
if any creature tells you that it hungers,
feed it.
If it tells you that it is dirty,
clean it.

If it cries to you that it hurts,
if you can,
ease its pain.

From the back garden you will be able to see the
    wild wood.
The deep well you walk past leads to Winter's
    realm;
there is another land at the bottom of it.
If you turn around here,
you can walk back, safely;
you will lose no face. I will think no less of you.

Once through the garden you will be in the
    wood.
The trees are old. Eyes peer from the under-
    growth.
Beneath a twisted oak sits an old woman. She
    may ask for something;
give it to her. She
will point the way to the castle.
Inside it are three princesses.
Do not trust the youngest. Walk on.
In the clearing beyond the castle the twelve
    months sit about a fire,
warming their feet, exchanging tales.
They may do favors for you, if you are polite.
You may pick strawberries in December's frost.

Trust the wolves, but do not tell them where
   you are going.
The river can be crossed by the ferry. The ferry-
   man will take you.
(The answer to his question is this:
If he hands the oar to his passenger, he will be free to
   leave the boat.
Only tell him this from a safe distance.)

If an eagle gives you a feather, keep it safe.
Remember: that giants sleep too soundly; that
witches are often betrayed by their appetites;
dragons have one soft spot, somewhere, always;
hearts can be well-hidden,
and you betray them with your tongue.

Do not be jealous of your sister.
Know that diamonds and roses
are as uncomfortable when they tumble from
   one's lips as toads and frogs:
colder, too, and sharper, and they cut.

Remember your name.
Do not lose hope—what you seek will be found.
Trust ghosts. Trust those that you have helped
   to help you in their turn.
Trust dreams.
Trust your heart, and trust your story.

Neil Gaiman

When you come back, return the way you came.
Favors will be returned, debts be repaid.
Do not forget your manners.
Do not look back.
Ride the wise eagle (you shall not fall)
Ride the silver fish (you will not drown)
Ride the gray wolf (hold tightly to his fur).

*There is a worm at the heart of the tower; that is
why it will not stand.*

When you reach the little house, the place your
    journey started,
you will recognize it, although it will seem
    much smaller than you remember.
Walk up the path, and through the garden gate
    you never saw before but once.
And then go home. Or make a home.

Or rest.

Neil Gaiman says: "When I was a small boy, my favorite fairy tale was probably 'Snow White.' I would stare, fascinated, at apples that were red on one side and green on the other, and wonder how you poisoned just half an apple, and whether the red half really did taste better than the green half. And it left me with a fondness for wicked and magnificent witch-queens that, it only occurs to me now, is probably why I put one in *Stardust*, my latest book, which is a fairy tale for adults.

"'Instructions' is, quite literally, that: It's a tale of what to do when you find yourself in a fairy tale. It's always best to be prepared for these things, after all."

Gaiman is also the author of the Sandman series of graphic novels and of the novel *Neverwhere*. He lives in Wisconsin.

Mrs. Big:

"Jack and the Beanstalk" Retold

by Michael Cadnum

Sometimes I complained too much, but there was a lot to complain about.

We couldn't live in the village among the joiners and the potters. We shook the ground when we tiptoed, and every time we napped in the town square we rolled over and crushed the Charter Oak or the Stone of Justice, or some other ancient monument beloved by man and boy. Our burps shattered windows in the chapel, and my stifled sneezes slopped duck ponds dry.

I started telling him it was all the fault of the peewee Englishmen, so tiny, their yells were squeaks. I flattened an ox by mistake one morn, out shaking dust off a doily. The ox-drovers cried out in terror, bovine mush all over my instep. "The Englishmen are too small," I said. "And not only that, the Englishmen are thieves!" This was the truth, as all giants know. Our kind always have some few tons of gold dust or silver nuggets tucked away. And we were always brushing away a couple of carter's boys or tanner's apprentices—trying to steal our nodes of ore.

One evening out watching the full moon come up, I trod on a milkmaid, and I knew then we had to make changes. It was bad enough having to scrub girl-juice off my best wooden shoe. It was the way my husband took it so hard that really troubled me. He brooded for days on why people-folk are so minuscule and easy to squish. And as tough as I like to sound, I don't like squashing maidens any more than you would.

Little by little his usual complacent, happy nature started to go sour. Before, he had been glad to wave at a passing farmhand. Now he frowned, and stuck out his lip, and started the beginnings of his famous poem. "I smell an Englishman," he would say, a picnic of villagers scrambling out of his shadow. "I smell the blood of an Englishman," he would say, shaking his fist, which was the size of a cow barn.

I encouraged him. "You smell the blood of a mite, is what you smell," I said. "A bunch we'd be well rid of." They had a strong scent: charred beef and tobacco, green ale and cheddar. You could nose a gentleman farmer and his lady half a league away.

I had hoped my beloved would be one of the Raving Giants, terrors of the earth, and devour the citizens of the countryside, like my great uncle, scourge of Europe. I'd hoped he'd be a Bard of the Big, like a few of my

36   Michael Cadnum

forebears. But, instead, he was a garden-giant, planting oaks and patting the earth around their roots. He had fine gold in bags of whale skin stitched together, and silver in schooner sails, but otherwise he was more peaceful planter than monster.

One day he hurried home with a gleeful expression, poplars shivering at his tread. He announced, in a voice loud enough to give a flock of passing geese a collective heart attack, "I've found a home!"

He'd bought it from a traveling peddler for a pocketful of pumpkins, he explained. It was acreage with a view, a mansion, plenty of garden space, but one drawback from the point of view access: It was in the clouds.

What sort of peddler? I thought to ask, but could not get the words out in my wonderment.

We had to stack carriages, oxcarts, sheds, and steeples one on top of each other, a teetering column, just so we could clamber up and take possession of the place. Once there, the pile tumbled back to earth with a dusty crash, and we were homeowners.

What sort of peddler indeed! I had cause to think in days and weeks to come. If I walked beyond where the wash was hanging, blue and yellow in the sun, I'd stumble and there it would be, the land way down there, cloud spinning off right under my feet. We feasted on gourds, squash, marrow, courgettes, that race of veggies that grows big. When the cloud-land parted, some of the yams tumbled down, all the way to the countryside below.

Mrs. Big

My husband would patch the cloud-field with some more of the stuff we walked around on, and rake it neat.

The view from the mansion was all thunderhead and sun, and sometimes a bird would make it all the way up to where we lived. He would alight on one of the melon plants that grew like weeds and peep around at things, bright and chirpy. I was learning to be a wiser giantess, and learned not to complain so much, even when my husband made up more of his poem, the verses of which could get on even a stone saint's nerves.

"I smell the blood of an Englishman," he would say, and then try out the words, "Peas, cows, drakes, drums, I smell the . . ." Or other random word assortments, until I wanted to scream. My father was the Giant Poet of the East, renowned among the deepest valleys for his alliterative verse. He's the wit who made up such famous phrases as *shilly-shally, hale and hearty, vim and vigor,* and other such word-pairs.

I explained the importance of form over meaning, of nonsense over simple declaration, and my husband, the poor dear, took it so to heart, he sulked. This pained me, because the truth is I was growing very fond of my huge hubby, isolated in the sky though we were.

His earnest humming in the cuke patch, his merry "Blood of an Englishman" yodel, all worked him ever deeper into my heart. I came to regret that I'd ever been critical in the first place. So when he burst in on me as I darned his breeches, and blurted out, "I smell the blood

Michael Cadnum

of an Englishman! Fee, Fie, Foe, Fum!" I clapped with appreciation, and patted his pink cheek.

I should have kept my mouth shut. "But wouldn't it be better back to front?" I began. And when he beamed, uncomprehending, I continued, "With the 'Fee, Fie' part first in the poem, the 'blood' part second?"

Such a sulk I have never observed in man or giant, a sulk of such deep duration, I was afraid he would never speak again.

Long days and somber nights he tugged the weeds, watered the crookneck and the summer squash with squeezed cloud, wrung out like sponges on the leafy vines. He met my eyes with sorrow, bearing up, brave-hearted, but thinking he had failed me, knowing how my family prized a turn of phrase. So there we were, solemn and quiet, when the terrible thing happened.

One day I was wringing the suds from my husband's knickers, and the next a human flea was squeezing through a hole in the cloudy field. Not one of the usual wear-and-wind holes, either, but a puncture made by a bean vine with leaves as big as me. I couldn't scream, I couldn't take a breath.

The lad was quick, and like a weevil he crept along the garden path, but by then my husband straightened in the garden, sniffing. Sniffing the bright air, he said softly, "Fee, Fie, Foe, Fum. I smell the blood of an Englishman." Gentle, like it was a love poem, an offering from his heart. Then he frowned. "I do!" he exclaimed. "I smell—"

He gathered himself, put one foot forward, and sang out, for all under the sky to hear, "Fee! Fie!" And continued on to declaim his entire, famous poem, the one they heard from Iceland to Crete that very instant.

We couldn't find the boy. The human pup got lost in the hall, and lost in the pantry, and lost in the parlor, too. All over the mansion we sniffed him out, but not a glimpse could we see.

Human as he was, I should have known. A giant's footstool, a god-sized spoon, a magnificent pair of breeches drying over a chair the size of a county were nothing to an English lad. He sought gold. He squirted through the chest-chamber, leaped up the side of a cask of gold, and bounded high, onto a sack the side of a guild house. He was a leaping-lad, digging and cutting with a cunning little knife, gold dust like summer wheat pouring out upon the floor.

He stuffed his breeches pockets with as much gold as he could cram, and leaped more slowly, jumped and scrambled. And then he stumbled, weighed down with twenty-four-carat powder, and rolled under my feet. In my fear that I might flatten him dead on the spot, I lifted one foot. I shifted another. I swayed.

I swung my arms, and fell with a crash that shook the cloud-land and shivered the billowing cumulus from north to south. My husband caught my look of pain, his eyes filled with shock at my distress, and ran after the human speck, bellowing the poem.

Michael Cadnum

The thief was clumsy, fat with gold, escaping the grasp of my angry spouse by a feather's span. I hurried after the two, gasping that I was not hurt, but now, when I wished my words had weight, they had no effect on large or small. The thief heaved himself to the stalk and shimmied down, leaf to leaf, falling, catching himself, until he was out of sight.

My husband hesitated—no giant can scramble, or bound, or spring to save his life. He took a deep breath and clambered down behind him, swaying the mighty beanstalk, leaves thrashing, covering the sound of my cry that I was all right, that my loved one need not avenge me. The thief had scampered all the way down to the landscape before my husband had mastered his grip on the leaves, and the thief began to work with a tiny ax, far below.

Who has not heard the story? How my husband fell, crashing through the green into the flat and distant earth? How Jack—for even robbers have names— hugged his mum and bragged of gold, and three beans exchanged with a peddler for a cow. While my husband lay like a hill, a mountain shaped like a man, stretched out with his last glance bright with love for me.

Fear not, Jack and Jack's mother, I wanted to say. Stay calm, villagers and geese. I sought no vengeance on a foolish lad, or harm to roof or heath. And be not afraid of my story's end, or believe it tells the demise of my beloved.

Even then I spied the creature I wanted, stealing down the hedgerows, the single cause of all my grief. I hurried after him, my shadow flowing ahead of my stride.

Sorcery that can ennoble the clouds with an estate, and sprout a beanstalk to heaven from three beans, can cure a giant poet of a fall. I sought the scurrying peddler with his magic wares.

He ran across a cow pasture, fled across a barnyard, staggered through daisies.

And I followed easily, bending, reaching. He was far too slow.

Michael Cadnum

Michael Cadnum has always been interested in stories about giants, and he thinks "Jack and the Beanstalk" is one of his favorites. Not only did the story have a very impressive giant, but it had a secret landscape in the clouds, which is another fascinating subject. He thinks we have all seen mountains and valleys in the clouds from time to time. What a wonderful kingdom for a giant the sky would be....

Michael Cadnum's novel about Robin Hood, *In a Dark Wood*, was chosen by the Smithsonian as one of 1998's best books for young people. His most recent novels are *Heat* and *Rundown*.

Falada:

The Goose Girl's Horse

by Nancy Farmer

My troubles began when the queen of Elfland put Conrad on my back. As a fairy horse I was used to strange riders. The queen often asked me to carry royal guests. *Asked* me, you understand. I was no bumbling farm horse. The queen would say, "*Dear* Falada. Would you mind taking this dwarf (or gnome or goblin) for a tour of the royal gardens!"

And I would say, "Of course!" unless it was a goblin. Some of them like to chew on ears.

I was a beautiful mare. I had silvery-white hair and a long, silver mane. My golden horseshoes were fastened with diamond nails, and when I galloped, sparks flew up from my feet. Right in the middle of my forehead was a gray circle. It was exactly where a horn would have grown, if I'd been a unicorn. My great-grandfather on my mother's side *was* a unicorn.

So you see I was no ordinary horse. And when the

queen put Conrad on my back—without asking!—I was insulted. First, I should explain about Conrad. He was a human child. Every now and then the elves carry off a baby they find interesting. They call it *borrowing*, but I call it *stealing*. They keep this child until they get bored with it. Then they return it to the poor mother.

By that time the child has learned bad habits. The elves spoil it rotten. They feed it candy instead of fruit, never send it to bed on time, and give in to it every time it throws a temper tantrum. And believe me, those brats know how to throw tantrums.

Conrad was eight years old and no longer cute. The queen was tired of his screaming fits, so she put him on my back and said, "Take him around the garden. Don't throw him off, either. I know your tricks."

She was annoyed at me because I had dumped a pair of gnomes into a rosebush the week before. I couldn't see what the fuss was about. Everyone knows gnomes bounce. I trotted off with Conrad clinging to my mane. His fingers were sticky with chocolate.

"Don't hang on to me," I said.

"Make me stop," jeered Conrad.

"Good riders hold on with their knees," I explained patiently.

Conrad gave a vicious tug to my mane. "I could pull this out," he said. "I could stuff a pillow with it."

"You already have a pillow," I told the little monster.

"Maybe I want another one." He yanked so hard, I

saw stars. I actually felt a clump of my beautiful, silver mane being torn out! I stopped short, kicked up my heels, and tossed Conrad into the thorniest rosebush in the garden.

You could hear him scream all the way to the goblin king's palace in the mountains. He was only bleeding in a dozen or so places, but the queen was furious. "I'm sick of all the noise around here," she cried. "You, Falada, will be given a task among humans. If you do it well, I *might* let you return. And you, Conrad, are going straight back to your mother."

I felt sick. I was being banished from Elfland. Every now and then a fairy animal is given a task in the real world. That's where all those magic foxes, firebirds, and talking fish come from. The task is always unpleasant.

An Elf lord put a rope around my neck and took me along the misty road that leads to the real world. The first thing I noticed was the dirt crunching beneath my feet. Then I felt my first horsefly bite. The sun was too hot, the grass too dry, the water too muddy.

I saw myself in a stream. My golden horseshoes were gone. My silver hair had turned gray. Oh, woe, woe, woe! I was no better than a mangy plow horse on a turnip farm.

My task was to carry the princess Belinda to her future husband in the next kingdom. "Watch over her," whispered Belinda's mother, who knew I was a fairy horse. "She's a sweet girl, but rather foolish." The

Nancy Farmer

old queen sighed. "I suppose I babied her too much."

My heart sank when I saw Belinda. She was a soft, pretty child. She cried when a bird flew into the courtyard and snapped up a grasshopper. "Do something," she wept, wringing her hands.

"There, there," said the old queen. "The bird is only taking food home to her babies."

We started out. I walked carefully with the princess Belinda on my back. Behind me came a handsome black horse with Belinda's serving maid, Dagmar. Belinda clapped her hands when she saw anything new. Everything was a delight to her. She liked the trees and the squirrels that chattered at us from the branches. Every flower filled her with joy.

Dagmar, on the other hand, hated everything. She thought squirrels were only good for squirrel pie, and that trees should be chopped up for firewood. "This forest is probably full of bears," she sniffed.

"How I'd love to see a cuddly, wuddly little bear! Do they really drink honey?" cried Belinda.

"They eat people and drink blood," said Dagmar.

That shut Belinda up for a while, but soon she was warbling again. Everything was new to her, you see. She was a kind, happy girl.

When we got to the first stream, Princess Belinda said, "Dear Dagmar, could you bring me a cup of water?"

"Get it yourself. You aren't lame," said Dagmar.

"Don't let her get away with that," I told Belinda.

"You're going to be a queen someday. You must learn to give orders." But the girl was too afraid. She climbed down from the saddle and fetched her own water.

Later in the day we came to another stream. "Dearest, dearest Dagmar. Would you mind *terribly much* getting me a cup of water?" asked Princess Belinda.

"Of course I mind *terribly much*," said Dagmar. So the princess climbed down and fetched her own water.

That night Dagmar refused to cook dinner or wash dishes or make up beds. Each time, I told the princess, "Don't let her get away with that." And each time, Belinda wrung her hands and cried.

I gave up and joined the black horse under a tree. "Things aren't working out at all," I muttered to myself.

"Things are working out fine," the black horse replied.

I was amazed. Another talking horse! "Are you from Elfland?" I asked.

"Hardly. My mistress and I come from the goblin king's palace in the mountains."

So that explained it. Dagmar was a goblin. No wonder she was so angry and rude.

In the morning, Dagmar made Belinda take off her beautiful golden dress and put on rags. She smeared Belinda's face and hair with mud. "There! No one will ever know you're a princess. If you tell on me, I'll chop you into little pieces. And if *you* tell on me, Falada, I'll have your head cut off." Neither Belinda nor I doubted her for a second.

Dagmar put on the golden dress. When we got to the neighboring kingdom, the old king and his son Humbert came out to greet us. Prince Humbert was delighted with Dagmar. "You're more beautiful than I expected," he cried.

"And you're dumber than I expected," said Dagmar with a sweet smile. Prince Humbert didn't even care that she had insulted him. He had fallen head over heels in love with her. He was the kind of prince who liked being pushed around.

"What shall we do with your serving maid?" asked the old king.

"Oh, her! She's so foolish, she's only good for herding geese," sneered Dagmar.

So Belinda was taken off to a goose farm, and I was chained to a millstone at a mill. Round and round I trudged, grinding grain into flour. My hooves wore down from all the walking. My tail became tangled and full of burrs, and my bones stuck out under my dusty, dirty skin. I looked *worse* than a mangy plow horse on a turnip farm.

Every day Belinda came by with a herd of geese. With her—I could hardly believe it—was Conrad, who had got me into trouble in the first place. His mother had hired him out to the goose farmer. "Hello, Falada. You look awful," the little monster said happily.

"*Geese, geese, hiss and fight. Give Conrad a nasty bite,*" I chanted. I might be banished, but I was still a fairy horse. I knew a little magic. The geese flapped their wings and nipped Conrad's behind. He ran off screaming loud enough to be heard in the goblin king's palace in the mountains.

"Poor Falada, you look so unhappy," sighed Princess Belinda.

"You, too," I said.

"*Alas, alas, if mother knew, I fear her heart would break in two,*" the princess said. "I'd better get these geese to the meadow before they get into more mischief." She herded them onward with a little switch cut from a willow tree.

As time passed, I noticed a change in Belinda. She no longer wrung her hands and wept. In fact, Belinda was learning a great many things from the goose farmer and the goose farmer's wife. Now she could bake bread and grow vegetables. She could shear a sheep and take an egg away from a hen without getting pecked. The more Belinda learned, the more confident she became.

Every day she came past the mill yard and brought me a bunch of carrots or an apple. I, in turn, taught her how to get rid of Conrad. He had a habit of pulling out strands of her long, golden hair to make fishing lures. Now, when he crept up on her, she chanted, "*Blow, wind, with all your might. Blow Conrad's hat right out of sight.*" He spent the rest of the afternoon running all over the meadow after his hat.

Finally, though, Conrad got angry. He waited outside the back door of the palace until the old king came out to sun himself in the garden. "Sir! Sir!" the boy called. "Please listen to me, sir!"

The old king had twelve sons and liked children. "Come here, lad," he said kindly. "What's your problem?"

"It's that nasty goose girl," said Conrad. "Every day she does a magic trick. She has the wind blow my hat all over the meadow. She talks to a horse, too, *and it talks back*. I think she's a witch, sir."

"Well, well. A talking horse. That's something I have to see," said the old king.

Early the next morning he came to the mill yard and sat on a stone. He was dressed like a farmer, but I knew exactly what he was. You don't grow up in Elfland without learning who's a king and who isn't.

Quite soon Belinda came by with her herd of geese. Conrad was bouncing up and down with pure glee. He saw the old king on the stone. "Poor Falada, you look so unhappy," sighed the princess.

"You, too," I replied.

"Alas, alas, if mother knew, I fear her heart would break in two."

Then the devil got into me. *"Geese, geese, hiss and fight. Give Conrad a nasty bite,"* I chanted. Straight off, the geese flapped their wings and nipped Conrad's

Falada   51 behind. He ran off screaming loud enough to be heard in the goblin king's palace in the mountains.

The old king laughed so hard, he almost fell off his stone. "That's something you don't see every day," he wheezed. "Come on now, you two. Tell me how a fairy horse and a most unusual goose girl landed in my backyard."

But both Belinda and I were afraid to speak. We knew Prince Humbert was married to a goblin. Belinda didn't want to be chopped into pieces, and I didn't want my head cut off. "Well, sir, it's difficult to say," I began.

"We promised not to tell," said Belinda.

The old king looked from one of us to the other. "I see you are afraid. Well, well. I don't know what to do about that."

Suddenly Belinda straightened her backbone. "I'm through with being a coward," she said. "I've stayed up all night with the lambs when they were sick. I've brought horses to the barn during a thunderstorm. *They* were frightened, but I didn't have time for it."

"Spoken like a true princess," said the old king, smiling.

So then Belinda told him about the trip through the forest and how she was forced to change clothes with the goblin. The old king stood up in a towering rage. He strode off to the palace, calling for his guards, his soldiers and his executioner.

But by the time he got there, Dagmar was gone. In

Nancy Farmer

the way goblins have of knowing when to flee, Dagmar had saddled up her handsome black horse and taken off for the mountains as fast as she could go. Oh, and she took Prince Humbert with her. He was still in love with her, goblin or not. Besides, he liked the way she ordered him around.

Princess Belinda married his little brother Prince Herkimer instead. He was second in line and had a much better character.

I was allowed to return to Elfland. As I crossed over the border, my cracked hooves became smooth again. My hair turned from gray to silver, and my skin became sleek and fat. "It's great to be back," I sighed. When I got to the queen's palace, I saw she had visitors.

They were Dagmar, Prince Humbert, and that wickedly handsome black horse. Dagmar had changed, too, when she crossed over the border to Elfland. She looked exactly like a goblin, which meant she was pea green and had a fine pair of tusks on either side of her nose.

"Things worked out after all," I told the black horse.

"Well, of course," he snorted. "Your job was to take the princess to her new kingdom. *My* job was to see she got some sense before she became a queen. You weren't the only one who was given a task." And we went off to the garden together before anyone could ask us for a ride.

Nancy Farmer grew up in a hotel on the Mexican border. She relates that "the hotel patrons—retired railroad men, cowboys, circus performers, and bank robbers on vacation—stayed up all night, gossiping and playing cards. They were so entertaining, I never got to bed before 3 A.M. and fell asleep in school the next day. I was a terrible student. In sixth grade I learned how to play hooky. I ran away so often, my teachers used to say, 'Who are you?' whenever I showed up.

"But I read mountains of books. I can't think of a fairy tale I *didn't* like. One of my favorites was 'Sleeping Beauty.' Every time I got to the part where the princess pricks her hand on the spindle, I cried, 'Don't take presents from old hags you find lurking in deserted towers! Didn't your mother teach you anything?' I was upset by fairy stories (and there are lots of them) where innocent animals were killed so the heroine could live happily ever after. In particular, I thought Falada the horse got a raw deal. How long did her head stay nailed over the gate? Who did she talk to? How did she eat?"

As an adult, Farmer ran a chicken farm in India, controlled insects on traffic islands in California, monitored water purity for villages in central Africa, and, last of all, wrote children's books. Her novels are *Do You Know Me*; *The Ear, the Eye and the Arm*; *The Warm Place*; and *A Girl Named Disaster*; plus one picture book, *Runnery Granary*. *The Ear, the Eye and the Arm* won a Newbery Honor for 1994, and *A Girl Named Disaster* won a Newbery Honor for 1997 and was a finalist for the National Book Award.

A Wolf at the Door

by Tanith Lee

It was summer during the Ice Age, so Glasina wasn't at school. She spent her holidays with her father and mother in a large house by the sea, whose water in summer unfroze and turned to liquid, although the shore was still deep in snow. The sea and the sky were blue in summer, and the ice cliffs behind the house shone and sparkled. The tall trees in the snowfields put out leaves like glass, which tinkled. They had changed over the centuries of the Ice Age in order to survive, and their trunks were like thick sticks of hard, green sugar. Lions lived along the shore near the house, and they had had to change, too. The lions had developed long, heavy, grayish fur, and huge orange manes (to show they were still fierce), which from the front made them look like chrysanthemums.

For the first fortnight of the summer holidays, Glasina's mother, who was a teacher, was still away teaching in the south. But Glasina's father was an artist,

55

and he always worked at home in the house by the sea.

On the fifth day of her holiday, Glasina was walking along the snowy shore by the dark blue sea. She had her camera, and took pictures of the seals playing in the water, and of the lions, some of whom were fishing off the ice floes. The lions were used to Glasina, since she and her parents fed them sometimes.

After she had walked about a mile, and taken about twenty photographs, Glasina sat down on a snowdrift, and simply smiled and sighed at the joy of being on holiday. Then, when she turned her head, she saw a black wolf was trotting along the sea's edge, toward her.

Now Glasina knew that wolves were not often dangerous; if you acted sensibly, they would never attack you unless they were starving. But this wolf could be hungry, for it looked very thin, and its pale eyes gleamed. Glasina stood up and pointed her camera at the wolf, who might not be sure what it was.

"Stay where you are," said Glasina, "or I'll shoot."

"Shoot away," said the wolf carelessly. "Though I don't look my best."

Glasina lowered the camera. Because of the Ice Age, to help them survive most of the animals had learned how to talk, but usually they could only manage a few words. For example, the lions could only say things such as, *Hallo, wot ya got?* and *More!* This wolf, though, was different.

"How are you?" Glasina therefore said politely.

Tanith Lee

"Fine," said the wolf. "And that's a lie."

"Yes," said Glasina. "Have you had a difficult winter, wolf?"

"Terrible," said the wolf. It came and sat down nearby. "Is that your house?" it inquired.

'Well, it's my parents' house, but I live there."

"Wow," said the wolf. "Do you mean you're still at school? I thought you were at *least* eighteen."

Glasina was fourteen, and she wasn't silly, either. The wolf was obviously trying to get on her good side. On the other hand, her father and mother would expect her to be kind to the wolf, and considerate.

"If you'd like to come with me," said Glasina, "my father or I can get the food machine to make you something to eat."

"Oh, wonderful," said the wolf, rolling over in the snow with delight. "And I'd give *anything* for a bath! Do you know," it went on, hurrying at Glasina's heels, "I haven't slept in a proper bed for weeks."

"How's the wolf today?" asked Glasina's father three mornings later.

"Still in bed," said Glasina, "with the covers up over its ears. It's spilt coffee on the sheets again, too, and last night it left the bath taps running. The housework machine's still clearing up."

"I'm not happy about this," said Glasina's father, whose hands were red and blue from his latest painting.

"And your mother won't like it at all when she gets home."

Glasina had already taken a photo of the wolf in bed in the guest room in case it left before her mother returned and her mother didn't believe what had happened, and how it had broken two coffee mugs and two teacups, and about the egg stain on the living room wall—the wolf had been explaining how it had run away from some polar bears and brought down its foot in the fried eggs for emphasis. There were also some T-shirts the wolf had wanted to wear, one of which was Glasina's mother's favorite, and the wolf had torn all the T-shirts across the back when it was dancing to Glasina's music tapes, leaping and waving its paws.

"What shall we do?" said Glasina uneasily.

"To be honest," said her father, "I don't know. I mean," he added later as they walked along the shore to avoid the horribly loud way the wolf was by then playing their music center (it always found the tapes they liked the least and said it liked those the best). "It seems to have wandered for miles across the snow, hungry and lonely and forlorn. It doesn't seem to have any family, or any friends . . . although, I must say, I'm not all that amazed by *that*. Its behavior as a human being is dreadful, but it doesn't seem to know how to be a wolf." He frowned. "Which is what worries me the most."

"I've been thinking about that, too," said Glasina.

"You hear these stories," said her father.

Tanith Lee

They stood and stared out to sea gloomily. It was a beautiful day, sunny and bright, and the water looked like sapphire jelly, but this didn't cheer them up. Nor did the sight of one of the lions standing on the ice at the sea's edge. The lion, too, seemed anxious, or only bored. She was a lioness, so she didn't have a mane and didn't look like a chrysanthemum.

"It's such a responsibility," said Glasina's father. "And, besides, what about you?"

"I wanted to go to college," said Glasina sadly.

"Of course, he couldn't claim you for at least three years—"

Glasina felt like crying, but she bravely didn't. Her father, however, rubbed red and blue paint all over his face without realizing it.

What they were afraid of was that the wolf was really a young man under a spell. According to the stories, if Glasina kissed the wolf, the spell would break, and it would become a young man again. But if he was as annoying as a human being as he was as a wolf, Glasina wasn't keen on the idea. She would, naturally, as his rescuer, be expected to fall in love with him and set up house with him in due course, in the correct tradition. It always happened like that in the stories. And Glasina hadn't planned her life this way. She wanted to learn things, travel, teach, and paint and take pictures. On the other hand, how could she allow a young man to go on being trapped in a wolf body once she'd guessed what was wrong?

A Wolf at the Door   59

"I suppose," said Glasina at last, "I'll have to do it."

"I'm so sorry," said her father. "I wish I could think of another way. Perhaps we should wait until your mother gets here—"

But just then there was a crash of crockery from the house as another coffee mug dropped from the wolf's clumsy paws.

"At least if he's a young man," said Glasina, "he'll be able to hold a mug properly. I'd better go and kiss him now."

The wolf was coming out of the house as they arrived. It was wearing a Walkman, although the earpieces didn't fit in its ears, and any minute everything seemed likely to fall off into the snow and get broken.

Glasina strode up to the wolf, with her father marching behind. Behind him loped the lioness, who had recognized them and kept saying insistently, "Hallo, wot ya got?"

"Wolf," said Glasina, "I've considered carefully, and you'd better understand I don't want to. But I will."

"And just you watch yourself when she does," shouted her blue-and-red-faced father angrily at the wolf.

"Wot ya got?" the lioness put in, and barged past them.

Glasina kissed the wolf on the cheek.

The lioness kissed the wolf on the other cheek.

Tanith Lee

The Walkman fell off and got broken.

The wolf disappeared.

Glasina and her father looked round nervously, and there was a lion with a chrysanthemum mane, gazing at the lioness in surprise. "Funny," it said. "I thought I was meant to be a human being—oh, well. Knew I had friends here somewhere. Confused by the spell . . . anyone can make a mistake." Then it trod on the Walkman, nuzzled the lioness, and said fiercely to Glasina's father, "Hallo, wot ya got?"

"I'll get you a lovely big steak," said Glasina's father, beaming.

"And I'll take your photo," said Glasina. To her relief, both lions only looked puzzled.

Tanith Lee, who lives on the coast of England, has written a number of novels for children and young adults, including *The Dragon Hoard; Princess Hynchatti; Prince on a White Horse; Islands in the Sky; Black Unicorn; Gold Unicorn;* and *Red Unicorn;* and *Law of the Wolf Tower,* first of the Wolf Law trilogy.

She says, "Wolves are part of the landscape for so many fairy tales—moving pieces of the Forest Dark and Terrible. As a child, they scared me, but I loved them, too (the love persists). My mother started my trend of turning such stories around, even inside out, and the oddity of humor that true drama somehow invites. (Something wonderful and very serious is so often the best material for the send-up.) I was always very intrigued by the *changes,* too—the frog who is really a prince, the cat who is a princess . . . maybe we are all something also, something other than what the world sees when it looks at us. How many people, for example, look at a child and see 'only' a child."

Ali Baba and the Forty Aliens

by Janeen Webb

Alberto Barbarino hated his name. He blamed his parents. They should have *known* that naming him after his uncle Al would cause confusion. His uncle was big Al, so Alberto was little Al, or Ali for short. And with *Barbarino*'s being the best-known Italian restaurant in the whole Ballarat goldfields district, when he got to school it didn't take long for the kids in his class to start calling him Ali Baba, after that stupid story the teacher read to them. The nickname stuck. And here he was, ten years old and nearly an adult, still called Ali Baba, still refusing to waste his time with the kids who called him that. He didn't need them, with their skateboards and their trendy bikes and their private jokes. He had better things to do.

Ali was pretty much a loner. He read all the *Sandman* comics and talked his mother into buying him a supply of gothic black T-shirts and black jeans. He had a black jean jacket, too, though he was saving up to replace it with a leather one. Black, of course. An oversized pair of Doc Martens and a dangling silver earring in the shape of an ankh completed his outfit. With his glossy black hair spiked up with gel, and his wraparound black sunglasses making his pale skin look even paler against the black clothes, he looked pretty cool.

His older brother, Dean, said he looked creepy. Ali didn't care. He stayed away from the noise and bustle of the family restaurant where everyone was shouting and his horrible brother was forever giving him errands to run. He headed for the hills, pedaling his battered bike to the old goldfields country on the outskirts of town. He mostly avoided the historical tourist park, where busloads of crumpled visitors paid to go into a fenced-off area to get what the glossy brochures called the "Australian gold rush experience." This meant that people dressed up in 1850s costumes showed the tourists how to pan for gold in the creek, and when the tourists got hot and bored, they were taken to the tourist shop to buy little bottles with specks of gold in them. Ali thought it was stupid, especially the way the visitors wandered around the park with their cameras looking for kangaroos and koalas. Okay, so there were kangaroos hereabouts in the scrub, but they avoided the tourists,

Janeen Webb

too, and Ali knew that no one making *that* much noise was ever going to see one!

So Ali left them to it, and pedaled farther out of town to the overgrown parts of the goldfields, where the roads turned into dangerous little tracks that buses and cars couldn't drive on. Ali loved the silence of the old diggings, with their mullock heaps and abandoned mines and weirdly shaped rusting machinery. He spent most of his free time out there, fossicking among the ruins or panning in the creek. And he did find valuables from time to time—little nuggets or flecks of alluvial gold, which he sold to the tourist shop when he had enough to make it worthwhile. He even went out to the diggings at night, hoping for ghosts. But he never saw one, not even when he found the lumps that marked bush graves of long-forgotten people. Maybe they were too tired after all that digging to be bothered haunting their graves.

Ali thought he knew all the old mine sites. But this Saturday morning he stumbled across one mine he could have sworn wasn't there the week before. Or ever before, come to think of it. There was something wrong about the entrance to this particular disused gold mine. Sure it looked like it had been dug out the hard way, by pick and shovel. And it had the usual rough-hewn wooden framework, the usual rusted-through bit of corrugated iron across the entrance, the usual KEEP OUT sign slapped on it in drippy paint. But something looked wrong. It was too neat. There were crumpled cola cans and paper wrappers lying about, typical rubbish you'd expect someone careless to leave after a picnic. But the grass was trampled flatter than a couple of picnickers with a blanket could have left it. And the bush was quiet. Too quiet. Like the birds and animals were giving it a wide berth. And it smelled wrong—the dusty bush smell was overlaid with some chemical tang Ali couldn't put a name to.

He decided to investigate. He had his flashlight. He told himself he'd just take a peek. He wouldn't go too far in. He bent to pull aside the old iron cover across the entrance. It wouldn't budge. It looked flimsy, like all the others, but Ali couldn't make it move at all. He climbed up onto the earth mounded above the entrance tunnel and tried to loosen the iron from the top. Nothing happened. He gave it a good hard kick, which hurt his foot. But the cover didn't even vibrate. Ali's frustration was growing—he climbed back down and tried attacking the old iron with a heavy piece of timber from the abandoned pile. Nothing. Not even a dent. The tin even sounded wrong, kind of muffled. The entrance was sealed. And Ali couldn't see what was sealing it.

Then it happened. One minute he was alone in the little bush clearing, next there was the sound of feet. A lot of feet. Ali was terrified. He felt the blood drain from his pale face, felt his heart thumping loudly in his chest. He barely had time to scramble up the nearest tree before the first of the intruders came into view. Ali counted forty of them, and they were all carrying packs and bundles of various shapes and sizes.

Ali knew they were aliens. They couldn't be anything else. They weren't bug-eyed monsters or robots or anything; they looked right, but they felt wrong. Like those models you make up from pictures and diagrams that never quite come out looking like the real thing. These guys looked like humans, but they didn't act like humans. They weren't talking or looking about, just heading straight for the mine. They carried their heavy packages without effort, without even breaking into a sweat. Maybe they couldn't sweat.

The chemical smell was getting a lot stronger, and Ali hoped he wouldn't choke or cry, or faint from the effort of staying still in his tree. He didn't think forty aliens would be very gentle if they caught him spying.

The aliens walked right up to the mine entrance. The leader faced the barrier that had been giving Ali so much trouble, and softly said, "Keep In."

That old corrugated iron didn't make a sound—it just disappeared. Now you see it, now you don't. And Ali watched openmouthed as the aliens walked *through* it and into the mine tunnel beyond. The entrance stayed open a few minutes, shimmering a little. There was a faint ozone smell in the air.

Then the door reappeared, solid as ever.

Ali waited in his tree, too scared to come down. Just

as he was thinking he'd have to make a run for it, the door dematerialized again. He saw the strangers walk back into the clearing, without their bundles. When the last member of the group appeared, the leader turned and murmured, "Keep Out." And the barrier was back. The aliens left, as strangely as they had come, vanishing into the bush.

Ali was shaking as he climbed down, but was fascinated, too. He wondered if the password would work for him. There was only one way to find out. He faced the entrance and said, "Keep In."

The ozone smell came back, and the doorway opened. Ali was inside before he could think about it. He'd expected it to be dark, but he found himself in a softly lit chamber. The walls were lined with shelves of experimental-looking tubes and specimen jars and equipment. Maybe the aliens were collecting samples. He hoped they didn't include any live ones. A familiar gleam attracted his gaze, and Ali found himself looking at a whole basket full of very small gold nuggets. There was another basket of natural crystals of various types, and even more baskets of minerals he couldn't identify.

Ordinarily Ali wouldn't take what wasn't his, but he figured this stuff didn't properly belong to the aliens, either. And no one in authority would believe his story if he told them—which he wouldn't. The aliens would never miss a few bits and pieces out of this huge hoard.

So Ali decided to help himself. He was not greedy:

He quickly filled his pockets with the smaller nuggets, and hurried back outside. He turned to the entrance and breathed the words, "Keep Out," watching in relief as the doorway resumed its abandoned gold mine disguise.

Back at the restaurant, Ali sidled into the preparation area and borrrowed the kitchen scales to weigh his treasure. Then he hid the gold at the bottom of his underwear drawer and quickly returned the scales. He planned to sell the gold a little at a time, until he had enough to buy his leather jacket without inviting suspicion.

But the weighing pan had been a bit sticky, and a couple of flecks of gold stayed stuck on the bottom. And the person who had noticed was Dean, who was helping out in the kitchen because Saturday night was so busy.

And that's where the trouble started. Dean sauntered into Ali's room and said, "So how come you got so much gold, you got to weigh it? Who'd you steal it from?"

His voice was low and nasty. Ali felt his face growing hot. He tried to sound casual. "You spied on me. I found it at the diggings, if you must know," he said.

Dean's answer was to grab Ali and push him hard against the wall. His breath was hot and sour in Ali's face as he said, "Listen, creep, I know you're up to something, and if you don't let me in on it, I'll tell Dad he should take a look in your underwear drawer. Understand?"

Ali admitted defeat. He didn't expect Dean to believe

him about the aliens, but the gold was a powerful incentive. Dean was already dreaming about cars and clothes and how impressed those stuck-up girls would be.

Next morning, a reluctant Ali took Dean out to the alien's gold mine. It looked just the same as it had yesterday, and that lingering chemical odor told Ali that the aliens had been back. He wondered if they'd noticed anything.

He faced the door and muttered, "Keep In," half hoping it wouldn't open. But it did, and Dean was through the entrance like a shot. He was making a lot of noise. Dean *was* greedy—he'd brought a couple of backpacks to fill with whatever looked valuable, despite Ali's objection that he'd never be able to carry them back to the edge of the scrub, where they had to leave their bikes.

Ali tried one more time to warn Dean not to stay too long, and not to take too much. Dean's only response was, "If you're so scared, you can piss off home."

So Ali left, feeling miserable and betrayed.

And that was the last time he ever saw his brother.

When Dean didn't come home that night, Ali told his parents the truth. Then he told it again to the police, and again to the search and rescue team. They didn't believe the stuff about aliens and magic doors, so Ali didn't push it. But the rest was plausible enough. The small amount of gold that Ali showed them could easily have come from a disused mine, and the police reckoned

Ali might have stumbled across the spot where one of the old fossickers who worked the diggings was storing his findings. They expected some old guy to turn up and claim he'd been robbed.

Volunteers combed the bush for days, looking for Dean. His bike was right there where he'd left it, untouched. Ali imagined they'd find his brother trussed up in one of those alien specimen jars, or worse.

But they never found him, or the exact same mine entrance that Ali described. The trouble was, it *had* looked just like all the others, and everyone thought that Ali was too upset to remember exactly where it was.

There was a lot of fuss on TV for a few days, and all kinds of experts said how dangerous the old diggings were, full of hidden mine shafts that a kid could fall down and never be found. Ali's distraught family and the local volunteers kept searching long after the experts went home. In the end, the authorities just labeled Dean's disappearance "misadventure." And left it at that.

But the kids at school wouldn't let it drop. Alberto Barbarino was a star. He was interviewed on TV, and he had press clippings and everything. Suddenly everyone wanted to talk to Ali. And Ali surprised them all by being willing to retell his story dozens of times, though he still left out the parts about the aliens. He found he kind of liked having a lot of new friends, and being on the inside of the private jokes that he used to hate so much. And he didn't even notice that he was too busy hanging out with his friends to go back to the old diggings very often.

He got to keep the gold. No one else claimed it. Finders keepers.

And he bought his black leather jacket.

But he doesn't wear it much.

Janeen Webb

Janeen Webb is a writer and academic who teaches literature at Australian Catholic University, Melbourne, Australia. When she was growing up in Newcastle, New South Wales, she spent most of her time reading, and surfing at the local beach. She always loved fairy tales, especially the ones where young people outsmart the grown-ups. She especially loved the *Tales from the Thousand and One Nights*, which is why she wrote her Ali Baba story for this book.

She is cowinner (with Jack Dann) of the Aurealis Award for best short story for "Niagara Falling," and "Death at the Blue Elephant" was on the final ballot for both the HQ Short Story prize and the Aurealis Award in the fantasy section. Both stories were chosen for *The Year's Best Australian Science Fiction and Fantasy, Volume 2* edited by Jonathan Strahan and Jeremy Byrne. Webb is also coeditor of the groundbreaking Australian anthology, *Dreaming Down Under*.

Her most recent nonfiction book is *Aliens and Savages: Fiction, Politics and Prejudice in Australia*, cowritten by Andrew Enstice.

Swans

by Kelly Link

My name is Emma Bear, and I am eleven years old. I live on Black Ankle Road beside the Licking River. I live in a palace. My father is a king. I have a fairy godfather. This summer I read *The True Confessions of Charlotte Doyle* and learned how to make blue dye from a flower called woad. I have six brothers. My mother is dead. I'm in the seventh grade. My father remarried this summer. My favorite class is home ec. I love to sew. I make all my own clothes. My mother taught me how to sew. I can also knit, crochet, and quilt.

Yesterday my stepmother pointed her pinkie finger at my brothers and turned them all into swans. They were being too noisy. I'm never too noisy. I don't talk at all.

This year I was failing choir. I opened my mouth to sing, and nothing came out. I hadn't been able to say a word since my mother died. In my other classes, it was okay. Homework was okay. Math was okay, and English. Art was okay. I could write down answers on the blackboard. I carried around a pad of paper and a pen. You'd be surprised how often you don't actually have to say anything. Mostly if I just nodded, it was okay. But choir doesn't work that way. You can't sing by writing on a pad of paper. But nothing came out of my mouth when I opened it.

Last year I had lots of friends. This year I didn't have any. What happened in between? My mother died. I stopped talking. No more friends. Really, I've been too busy to have friends, I suppose.

When I first stopped talking, no one noticed. Not until Mom's funeral, when we were all supposed to stand up and say something. I stood up, but nothing came out when I opened my mouth. First my father sent me to see a psychologist. I just sat on her couch. I looked at pictures, and wrote down what they looked like. They all looked like flowers, or birds, or schnauzers. Then my fairy godfather came to the palace.

My fairy godfather is a little man with red hair. His name is Rumpelstiltskin. He was a friend of my mother's. He'd been away on business for a few months—he'd missed the funeral. His eyes were all red, and he cursed a lot. He'd loved my mother a lot. He sat with me for a long time, brushing my hair, and patting my hand.

Finally he said, "Well, you certainly don't have to talk until you want to. Keffluffle. Excuse my French. What a mess this is, Emma."

I nodded. I wrote down on my pad of paper, *I miss her*.

"Fudge, I do, too," my godfather said. "Excuse the French."

He tapped me on the nose gently. "You know your father is going to have to get married again."

I wrote, *I'll have an evil stepmother?*

"That evil stepmother stuff is just a pile of horsepucky," he said, "excuse me. It's just baloney. Whoever he marries will be just as afraid of you and your brothers as you are of her. You keep that in mind."

To my father, he said, "Emma just needs a piece of time. When she needs to say something, she'll open her mouth and say it."

He hugged my father, and he hugged me. He said, "I have a commission for you, Emma. I have a godchild who is going to a ball. All she's got to wear are rags. She needs a fancy dress. Not pink, I think. It wouldn't match. She's got lovely red hair, just like me. Maybe a nice sea-foam green. Right down to the ankles. Lots of lace."

I wrote, *When do you need it?*

"When she turns seventeen," he said. "That's not for a bit. I'll send you her measurements. Okay?"

Okay, I wrote and kissed him good-bye.

When my mother was young, she was famous. She could spin straw into gold. Her name was Cleanthea. A year ago, she went jogging in the rain, and then she caught cold, and then she died.

My mother's quilts were famous. Famous quilts have their own names. She made crazy quilts, which are just bits of scraps sewn together, and then decorated and embroidered with fancy stitches—wheat stitches, briar stitches, flowers, birds, little frogs, and snowflakes. She made Log Cabin quilts and Wedding Ring quilts, and she also made up her own patterns. Her quilts had names like Going Down to the River and Snakes Fall in Love and Watering the Garden. People paid hundreds of dollars for them. Every bed in the castle has a quilt on it that my mother made.

Each of my brothers had a quilt that my mother made just for them. She made my brother Julian a *Star Wars* quilt, with X-Wing Fighters and Death Stars. She made my oldest brother an Elvis quilt. Up close it's just strips and patches of purple cloth, all different patterns. But when you back away, you can see that all the bits of different colors of purple make up Elvis's face—his eyes, his lips, his hair. For my youngest brother, she made a Cats Eat Birds quilt. She sewed real feathers into the cats' mouths, and little red cloth-patch birds into their stomachs.

She never finished my quilt. We were working on it together. I'm still working on it now. I don't really want to finish it. In fact, it's gotten a little bit big for my bed. When I spread it out, it's almost as big as a swimming pool. Eventually, it will fill up my whole room, I guess. Every night now I sleep on a different bed in the castle, under a different quilt. I pretend that each quilt is a quilt that I have never seen before, that she has just finished making, just for me.

I should tell you about my father and my brothers. I should also tell you about my stepmother. My father is very tall and handsome, and also very busy with things like affairs of state and cutting ribbons at the grand openings of grocery stores and presenting awards to writers and musicians and artists and also going to soccer games and football games so that photographers can take his picture. That was how he met my stepmother. He was at the zoo, which had just been given a rare species of bird. He was supposed to be photographed with the bird on his shoulder.

When he arrived, however, the keepers were distraught. The bird had disappeared. Even worse, a naked woman had been found wandering around the grounds. She wouldn't say who she was, or where she came from. No one could find her clothes. The keepers were afraid that she might be a terrorist, or an anarchist, come to blow up the zoo, or kill my father. It would be bad publicity for everyone.

"Nonsense," my father said. He asked to meet the woman. The zookeepers protested, saying that this was a bad idea. My father insisted. And so my father's picture appeared in the papers, holding out his hand to a woman dressed in a long white T-shirt and a pair of flip-flops that one of the keepers got out of the lost and found. The picture in the paper was blurry, but if you looked closely you could see the look in my father's eyes. He looked like he'd been hit on the head. He looked like he was falling in love, which he was.

The woman, my stepmother, looked small and fragile in the photograph, like a Christmas tree ornament. She had long, feathered hair. The T-shirt hung on her like a tent, and the flip-flops were too big for her.

We still don't know much about my stepmother. She was from a faraway country, we thought, because she had a slight but unrecognizable accent. She was a little bit cross-eyed, like a Siamese cat. She never brushed her hair. It stuck up in points behind her ears, like horns. She was very beautiful, but she hated noise. My brothers made too much noise. That's why she turned them into swans.

They came and stood on the lawn this morning, and I fed them dried corn and bits of burnt buttered toast. They came back early, while my stepmother was still sleeping. They honked at me very quietly. I think they were afraid if they were loud, she'd turn them into something even worse. Snails, maybe, or toads.

Some of the other girls at school thought I was lucky to have so many brothers. Some of them said how handsome my brothers were. I never really thought so. My brothers used to pull my hair and short-sheet my bed, and they never helped with my homework unless I gave them my allowance. They liked to sit on top of me and tickle me until I cried. But when my mother died, they all cried. I couldn't.

My brothers' names are George, Theodore, Russell, Anthony, William, and Julian. George is the oldest. Theodore is the nicest. Anthony is the tallest. Russell has freckles, and he is allergic to milk. William and Julian are twins, and two years younger than me. They liked to wear each other's clothes and pretend that Julian was William, and William was Julian. The thing is, all of them look alike now that they're birds. They all look like twins.

My father told us that my stepmother didn't like noise. They got married at the beginning of the summer. We got to throw rice. We'd only seen my stepmother twice before—once in the newspaper picture, and once when my father brought her home for dinner. There were a lot of important people at that dinner. We ate in the kitchen, but afterward we stood in the secret passageway and spied through the painting that has the eyes cut out.

My future stepmother didn't eat much dinner, but she had three helpings of dessert. This is when I first became suspicious that she was magic—a witch, or else under an enchantment. Witches and people under spells, magic people, always have sweet tooths. My fairy godfather carries around sugar cubes in his pockets and stirs dozens of them in his coffee, or else just eats them plain, like a horse. And he never gets cavities.

When my father and stepmother came back from their honeymoon, we were all standing on the palace steps. We had all just had baths. The palace steps had just been washed.

My father and stepmother were holding hands. When they saw us, my stepmother let go of my father's hand and slipped inside the palace. I was holding up a big sign that said, WELCOME HOME, DAD. There wasn't any room on the sign for STEPMOTHER.

"Hey," my brother George said, "what did you bring me?"

"Anthony stole my rocket launcher," Russell said.

"It wasn't me," Anthony said, "it was Theodore."

"It was NOT me," Theodore said, and William and Julian said, "Emma made us brush our teeth every night."

Everyone began yelling. My father yelled loudest of all.

"I'd really appreciate it if you all tried to be quiet and didn't yell all at once. Your stepmother has a bad headache, and besides, she's very shy, and not at all used to loud children," he said, looking at my brothers. Then he looked at me. "Emma," he said, "are you still not talking?"

I took out my notepad and wrote *yes* on it. He sighed. "Does that mean 'yes, you are talking now,' or 'yes, you still aren't talking'?"

I didn't say anything. I just smiled and nodded. "Maybe you'd like to show your new stepmother around the castle," he said.

My stepmother was in the library, reclining on a sofa with a damp cloth over her eyes. I stood there for a bit, and then I tapped my foot some. She didn't move. Finally I reached down and touched her shoulder. Her eyelids fluttered.

I held up my pad of paper. I wrote, *I'm Emma. I don't talk.*

She sat up and looked at me. She wasn't very big. When she stood up, I bet that we would have been the same height, almost, except she was wearing pointy black shoes with tall heels to make her look taller.

I wrote, *Dad asked me to show you the castle.*

I showed her around the castle. I showed her the kitchen with the roasting spit that the dogs turn, and the microwave, and the coffeemaker. I showed her the ballroom, which is haunted, and the dungeon, which my father had converted into an indoor swimming pool and squash court, and I showed her the bowling alley which is also haunted, and the stables, and the upstairs bathroom, which has modern plumbing. Then I took her to my mother's room. The quilt on the bed was Roses and

Kelly Link

Cabbages Growing Up Together, all pieced together from old green velvet hunting coats and rose-colored satin gloves.

My new stepmother sat down on the bed. She bounced experimentally, holding her head. She stared at me with her slightly crossed eyes. "A nice bed," she said in a soft, gravelly voice. "Thanks, Emma."

My mother made this quilt, I wrote. *Her quilts are very valuable. Please be careful when you are sleeping.* Then I left her there on my mother's bed. The next day she turned George into a swan. He was practicing his saxophone.

George is my father's heir. George doesn't want to be king. George wants to be a saxophonist in a heavy metal band. I was listening to him in the ballroom. He isn't very good yet, but he likes to have an audience. I sit and listen to him, and he pays me five dollars. He says someday it will be the other way round.

I was embroidering the back of a blouse with blue silk thread. I was trying to embroider a horse, but it looked more like a crocodile, or maybe a dachshund.

My stepmother had been swimming in the pool. She was still in her bathing suit. She came into the ballroom and left puddly footprints all over the waxed and polished black walnut floor. "Excuse me," she said. George ignored her. He kept on honking and tootling. He smirked at me. "Excuse me," our stepmother said, a little bit louder, and then she pointed her pinkie finger at him. She flicked her pinkie up at him, and he turned into a swan. The swan—George—honked. He sounded surprised. Then he spread out his wings and flew away through an open window.

I opened my mouth, but of course nothing came out. I stared at my stepmother, and she shrugged apologetically. Then she turned and left, still dripping. Later that afternoon when Anthony set off Russell's rocket over the frog pond, my stepmother turned him into a swan, too. I was up in the tree house watching.

You're probably wondering why I didn't tell someone. My dad, for instance. Well, for one thing, it was kind of fun. My brothers looked so surprised. Besides, at dinner no one missed Anthony or George. My brothers are always off somewhere, camping with friends, or else sleeping over at someone else's house, or else keeping vigil in the haunted bowling alley. The ghost always shows up in the bowling alley at midnight, with his head in his hand. The pins scream when he throws his head down the lane.

My stepmother had three helpings of pineapple upside-down cake. After dinner, she turned Theodore and Russell into swans. They were banging down the grand staircase on tin trays. I have to admit this is a lot of fun. I've done it myself. Not turning people into swans, I mean, sliding down on trays.

I had to open up a window for Theodore and Russell. They honked reproachfully at me as I pushed them out over the windowsill. But once they opened up their wings, they looked so graceful, so strong. They flew up into the sky, curving and diving and hanging on a current of air, dipping their long necks.

How do you do that? I wrote down on my pad. My stepmother was sitting down on the staircase, looking almost ashamed.

"I don't know," she said. "It just seems to happen. It's just so noisy."

Can you turn them back? I wrote.

"What an excellent inquiry," she said. "I do not know. Perhaps and we shall see."

William and Julian refused, as usual, to brush their teeth before bedtime. Loudly. I told them, *Be quiet, or else.*

"Or else what?" Julian screamed at me, his face red with temper.

New stepmother will turn you into a swan.

"Liar," William said loudly. He said it again, even louder, experimentally. My stepmother, wearing pink flannel pajamas, was standing there, just outside the bathroom door. She stuck her head in, looking pained. Julian and William pretended to be afraid. They screamed and giggled. Then they pretended to be swans, flapping their arms. My stepmother waved her finger at them, and they sprouted wings. They sprouted feathers and beaks, and blinked their black beady eyes at her.

I filled up the bathtub with water, and put them in it. It was the first time they ever seemed to enjoy a bath. Even better, they didn't have any teeth to brush.

Then I put them outside, because I wasn't sure if they were house-trained.

The next morning I woke under my favorite quilt, the Rapunzel quilt, with the gray tower, and the witch, and the prince climbing up the long yellow braids. I ate breakfast and then I went outside and fed my brothers. I'd never had pets before. Now I had six. I tried to decide what I liked better, birds or brothers.

When I went back to get more toast, my father was sitting in the kitchen, reading the morning paper. He was wearing the striped purple bathrobe I'd made him for Christmas three years ago. Mom had helped with the cuffs. The hem was a little bit frayed. "Good morning, Emma," he said. "Still not speaking? Where are the rest of you, anyway?"

I wrote down, *New stepmom turned them into swans.*

"Ha," he said. "You're a funny girl, Emma. Don't forget. Today I'm dedicating the new school gymnasium. We'll see you about two-ish."

First there were speeches. I sat with the rest of my grade, in the bleachers, and looked at my new stepmother. I was thinking that the smart thing would have been to buy her earplugs. Whenever my principal, Mr. Wolf, put his mouth too close to the microphone, there

Kelly Link

was a squeal of feedback. My stepmother was looking pale. Her lips were pressed tightly together. She sat behind Mr. Wolf on the stage, beside my father.

Sorley Meadows, who wears colored lip gloss, was sitting next to me. She dug her pointy elbow into my side. "Your stepmother is, like, tiny," she said. "She looks like a little kid."

I ignored her. My father sat with his back straight, and his mouth fixed in a dignified, royal smile. My father can sleep with his eyes open. That's what my mother used to say. She used to poke him at state occasions, just to see if he was still awake.

Mr. Wolf finished his speech, and we all clapped. Then the marching band came in. My father woke up. My stepmother put her hand out, as if she were going to conduct them.

Really, the band isn't very good. But they are enthusiastic. My stepmother stood up. She stuck out her pinkie finger, and instead of a marching band there was suddenly a lot of large white hissing swans.

I jumped down out of the bleachers. How mortifying. Students and teachers all began to stand up. "She turned them into birds," someone said.

My father looked at my stepmother with a new sort of look. It was still a sort of being hit on the head sort of look, but a different sort of being hit on the head. Mr. Wolf turned toward my father and my stepmother. "Your Royal Majesty, my dear mademoiselle," he said, "please do not be alarmed. This is, no doubt, some student prank."

He lifted the little silver whistle around his neck and blew on it. "Everyone," he said. "Please be quiet! Please sit back down."

My stepmother did not sit back down. She pointed at Mr. Wolf. Mrs. Heliotrope, the French teacher, screamed suddenly. Mr. Wolf was a swan. So was Mrs. Heliotrope. And as I watched, suddenly the new gynasium was full of birds. Sorley Meadows was a swan. John Riley, who is someone I once had a crush on until I saw him picking his nose in the cloakroom, was a swan. Emma Valerie Snope, who used to be my best friend because we had the same name, was a swan. Marisa Valdez, the prettiest girl in the seventh grade, was a swan.

My father grabbed my stepmother's arm. "What is going on here?" he said to her. She turned him into a swan.

In that whole gymnasium, it was just me and my stepmother and a lot of swans. There were feathers floating all over in the air. It looked like a henhouse. I pulled out my pad of paper. I jumped up on the stage and walked over to her. She had just turned my whole school into a bunch of birds. She had just turned my father into a bird. She put her hand down absentmindedly and patted him on the top of his white feathery head. He darted his head away, and snapped at her.

I was so angry, I stabbed right through the pad of paper with my ballpoint. The tip of the pen broke off. I threw the pad of paper down.

I opened my mouth. I wasn't sure what was going to come out. Maybe a yell. Maybe a curse. Maybe a squawk. What if she turned me into a bird, too? "WHAT?" I said. "WHAT?"

It was the first word I had said in a whole year. I saw it hit her. Her eyes got so big. She threw her arm out, pointing her pinkie finger at me. I was pointing at her. "WHAT?" I said again. I saw her pinkie finger become a feather. Her arms got downy. Her nose got longer, and sharp. She flapped her wings at me.

She wasn't a swan. She was some other kind of bird. I don't know what kind. She was like an owl, but bigger, or maybe a great auk, or a kiwi. Her feathers looked fiery and metallic. She had a long tail, like a peacock. She fanned it out. She looked extremely relieved. She cocked her head to one side and looked at me, and then she flew out of the gymnasium.

"WHAT?" I screamed after her. "WAIT!" What a mess. She'd turned my family, my entire school into birds, and then she flew away? Was this fair? What was I supposed to do? "I want to be a swan, too! I want my mom!"

I sat down on the stage and cried. I really missed my mom.

Then I went to the school library and did a little

research. A lot of the swans came with me. They don't seem to be house-trained, so I spread out newspaper on the floor for them.

My fairy godfather is never around when you need him. This is why it's important to develop good research skills, and know how to find your way around a library. If you can't depend on your fairy godfather, at least you can depend on the card catalog. I found the section of books on enchantments, and read for a bit. The swans settled down in the library, honking softly. It was kind of pleasant.

It seems that to break my stepmother's pinkie spell, I need to make shirts for all of the birds and throw the shirts over their necks. I need to sew these shirts out of nettle cloth, which doesn't sound very pleasant. Nettles burn when you pick them. Really, I think linen, or cotton is probably more practical. And I think I have a better idea than a bunch of silly shirts that no one is probably going to want to wear again, anyway. And how are you supposed to sew a shirt for a bird? Is there a pattern? Down in the castle storerooms, there are a lot of trunks filled with my mother's quilting supplies.

I miss my mother.

Excuse me. I just can't seem to stop talking. My voice is all hoarse and croaky. I sound like a crow. I probably wouldn't have gotten a good grade in choir, anyway. Mrs. Orlovsky, the choir teacher, is the swan over there, on top of the librarian's desk. Her head is tucked under her wing. At least I think it's Mrs. Orlovsky. Maybe it's Mr. Beatty, the librarian. My father is perched up on the windowsill. He's looking out the window, but I can't see anything out there. Just sky.

I think I'm going to finish the quilt that my mother and I started. It's going to be a lot bigger than either of us was planning on making it. When I finish, it should be big enough even to cover the floor of the gymnasium.

It's a blue quilt, a crazy quilt. Silk, corduroy, denim, satin, velvet. Sapphire, midnight blue, navy, marine, royal blue, sky blue. I'm going to patch in white birds with wide white wings on one side, and on the other side I'm going to patch in little white shirts. When I finish, I'm going to roll it up, and then throw it over all the swans I can find. I'm going to turn them back into people. This quilt is going to be as beautiful as sky. It's going to be as soft as feathers. It's going to be just like magic.

Kelly Link writes, "When I was very little, I was obsessed with the big bad wolf. I didn't care that much for the three little pigs. I liked the huffing and puffing. In kindergarten I was Little Red Riding Hood in the class play, and the next year I was the troll under the bridge in *The Three Billy Goats Gruff.* I got to wear a white beard made out of white cotton balls.

"When I was old enough to read to myself, I loved *The Tinderbox,* where the soldier meets the three dogs whose eyes are as big as saucers, as dinner plates, as spinning wheels. I also loved *The Goose Girl,* although I was never satisfied with the ending. Before the princess becomes a goose girl, she has a talking horse. Afterward, she has a prince, but no horse. I did not feel that a prince was anywhere near as good as a talking horse. I still don't. Now I love the Russian fairy tales, where the witch Baba Yaga lives in a house that walks around on chicken legs. Now that's as good as a talking horse.

"I wanted to retell the story of the girl who makes shirts out of nettles for her brothers, who have been turned into swans by their wicked stepmother. I thought that in my version, the girl might want to be a swan as well. I would. But Emma Bear is much more practical than I am. She's also much better at sewing."

Link lives outside Boston, Massachusetts.

The Kingdom of Melting Glances

by Katherine Vaz

The shape of a bright red lily was on Rosa's cheek. A shadow of a lily had once fallen across her face and blushed to touch a girl so beautiful and decided to cling to her forever. This miraculous bloom made her as special as a walking garden, but her sisters laughed and called her "Lily Face"—full of bites and buzzing! Rosa thought that they were actually mosquitoes that had grown enormous.

Rosa's parents had met each other years before in Portugal, by the sea. One day, when she was a pretty young girl, Mother sat down at The Wall of Melting Glances near the waves, which roared up like teeth made of liquid glass. Father, a young man longing for adventure, approached, and when he looked at Mother, and she looked back at him, their bones melted, their hearts changed to red, thump-thumping puddles, and their skin melted.

It was a good thing that a wall was there, or else these two would have trickled right across the burning sand to drown in the waves! Little boats, with eyes painted on the prows, watched with approval and bobbed up and down on the surf as if they were over-joyed to see that once again The Wall of Melting Glances had worked its spell.

The lives of Mother and Father continued melting together. They moved to the Gold Country of California, the dry, yellow-green valley below the mountains. There was no buried treasure anymore in the town of Gold Hills, of course. Only restaurants called "Prospector's Diner" or "Eureka Café," and antique shops called "Treasure Bin." Or "Mother Lode." Sometimes tourists would go into a place and pretend to pan for gold in a fake stream or look at pictures of scruffy men with mustaches who had come to these foothills in the past. Nowadays, there were lots and lots of nice but ordinary homes. The only gold coin to be discovered was the round, golden sun that shone angrily every day, from the first scream of the loggers' trucks and traffic to the close of day, when the loggers and commuters returned in a silvery stream of cars.

Mother missed the magic wall where she had fallen in love with Father, and she ached for water, sweet or sour, dripping or crashing, the sound and fishy smell and blue-green look of it. She took to her bed ready to dry up like an autumn leaf.

Father, his heart breaking, remembered the story of

Katherine Vaz

the Scandinavian princess who had long ago married a Portuguese prince. The prince took his new bride to southern Portugal, where she was shriveling and dying because she missed the cool, white snow of her homeland. The prince loved her so much that he planted almond trees, and their white blossoms covered the ground like snow. His princess recovered.

Father planted hydrangeas, which are globe-shaped flowers that drink water like thirsty children. They are so full of water that they're really sponges pretending to be flowers. The petals are bright pink and purple. Father climbed onto the roof with an armful of hydrangeas and shook them so that they dropped a pink-and-purple waterfall past Mother's window.

Joy returned to her.

Mother and Father soon had three daughters—Isabel, Ana, and Rosa-with-the-lily-on-her-face.

Isabel and Ana were cruel to Rosa and dry like twigs. Their words were brittle, and they never bathed. Rosa, meanwhile, loved to find streams in the Gold Country and go swimming beneath the apple and fig trees.

One day the sisters discovered that their parents had melted completely away. Isabel, Ana, and Rosa waded into their parents' room, into water up to their knees. The ceiling and walls were damp, and the water was seeping out under the door to run down the street.

"They've decided to go back to the sea without us!" said Isabel, kicking at the water. "What nerve!"

"They left us with a rotting house!" said Ana. "I can smell the mildew already!"

"That's you that you're smelling!" said Isabel.

"They've finally melted from loving each other so much," said Rosa, "and this water is all of them and their tears of joy." She cupped her hands together and drank up some of her melted parents.

Isabel and Ana crackled and almost snapped in two from laughing. Now they were free to torment their youngest sister more than ever.

"Lily Face, Lily Face!"

"Hey, water-lily, hey dilly-dilly."

Rosa stopped going to Gold Hills High School because everyone began to dance in front of her like a talking insect, with her sisters the biggest praying-mantis cheerleaders of them all with glowing red eyes and green-twiggy limbs. Yes, she knew she had the mark of a big red lily on her face! And yes, no matter how much anyone teased her, she still believed that her parents had melted in a flood of love!

Rosa stopped swimming in streams because the buzzing and teasing followed her there. She set a basin of cold water on her parents' windowsill, because she could not survive without little lakes or streams, even if they had to be make-believe ones. She watered the hydrangeas and looked out at the cloudless, huge sky of the Gold Country.

She knew that ghosts wandered across the gentle

curves of the valley, ghosts of the gold miners who had come here to seek their fortunes but who had now disappeared. Deep in the ground, their skeletons tried to dance under the weight of so much dirt. Rosa wished she knew the stories of the fortune-seekers. She wanted to unbury their pickaxes, their buckets and dirt-plastered blue jeans and weighing pans. And if she could, she would step in and settle the quarrels that had led to fights in the saloons . . . but that was all dissolved and vanished, sunk into the town and below the housing developments of Gold Hills the way that water sinks invisibly into a field of yellow grass.

She wept for her parents, though she knew they were happy.

One afternoon, a hummingbird lit down into the basin of water she kept at the window and beat his wings faster than most people can think a thought. He churned like a miniature water mill and splashed the lily on Rosa's face until she smiled. "There!" said the bird. "Why so sad?"

"Because I'm all alone," said Rosa.

"I was drawn to the lily on your face to drink from it, and then I saw that you had made a private swimming pool for me!"

"Yes," said Rosa, cheering up. "May I take hold of your wings and fly away with you?"

"Naturally," said the hummingbird.

But right as Rosa was preparing to take hold of the

bird's fluttery fairy-wings, her sisters saw what was happening and rushed in to slap the bird away.

They had no idea how swift hummingbirds are.

He sang out, "I'll return tomorrow!" to Rosa before he escaped.

"Will you deny me every comfort?" shouted Rosa at her sisters.

"If anyone should fly away on wings of joy, it should be us!" yelled the twig-sisters.

"A bird should collect you both to build a rotting nest!" shouted Rosa.

That night she set out a basin for the hummingbird once again. While Rosa slept—with her dreams the color of irises, lilies, roses, and sunflowers—Isabel and Ana tiptoed in and put razor blades all through the water.

Sharp razor blades! The twig-sisters went off to sleep a sound sleep, with only a blank where most people have dreams!

When the hummingbird returned in the moonlight and began to splash and bathe, the razor blades cut him terribly. He made a high-pitched sound that no human could hear. He flew away as best he could, badly injured, one wing almost completely cut off. Though his heart was only the size of a pinhead, it rattled like an alarm clock inside him. The next morning, when Rosa ran to the basin, she saw the blood in the water and wept so much that the water turned from red to pink.

Isabel and Ana pretended to know nothing, but Rosa

Katherine Vaz

was not fooled. She said to herself, I must be brave enough to leave this place and find him. If my princely bird is wounded, I shall nurse him back to health. If he is dead—and here she stopped to sob again—then I shall give him a proper burial.

Rosa remembered her mother saying that Portuguese people once believed that certain hours of the day are "open" or full of invisible doors, that a person can slip into another world if he or she believes in magic. Sometimes these open hours are at dawn, when the sun is still half asleep; sometimes at noon, when the sun tires for a moment of the endless day ahead; often at night, when the moon rides high, dropping its white flowers of light onto the landscape.

That evening, with her sisters snoring in another room, Rosa stepped through a silver door of moonlight and saw a thread hanging down from the moon like a white vine. She had scarcely reached up to touch it before it wrapped around her and hoisted her toward the mottled face of the Moon.

"You've got marks on your face, just as I do!" she cried to the Moon.

"Yes," said the Moon. "Mine are so huge, you can see them from Earth!"

"Moon, have you seen a hummingbird injured by razor blades planted by my horrible sisters?"

"No," said the Moon. "He might have been carried away on the Wind. Go, but take this gift."

The Moon wrapped a golden veil around her hair.

Rosa sailed away until a star punctured the moonlight, and she tumbled into the blue curving arms of the Wind.

"Wind, have you seen a hummingbird injured by razor blades planted by my horrible sisters?" she asked the Wind.

"I've tried to rip your sisters' hair out many times," said the Wind, sighing heavily, "but I have not seen the hummingbird. He might have been rescued by the Sun. Go, but take this gift."

The Wind blew a garland of golden grasses around her wrists as bracelets.

A blue shaft of wind carried Rosa along until a burst of sunlight cracked the blueness wide open and dropped her into the Sun's palace.

The gold on all sides shone so brilliantly that it went from gold to white-gold to white. The glare was so strong that sometimes it erased everything in its path, as if a painter had taken a cloth dipped in turpentine and wiped away part of the world. When Rosa stared at the palace floor, its dazzling golden squares made her dizzy. Even the lilies in the sun's garden were covered with gilt.

Rosa heard a sound, and turned her head to watch: A drawbridge made of gold dropped down, over a moat filled with sparkling golden water and golden crocodiles. Rosa could not tell where the sky ended and the teeth of crocodiles began.

Katherine Vaz

The Sun's Mother strolled out of the palace wearing a sun-bleached white dress.

"Have you seen a hummingbird injured by razor blades planted by my horrible sisters?" Rosa asked.

"Yes," said the Sun's Mother, "but he is in the high tower, and my son refuses to let anyone see him."

"Oh, but I must!" shouted Rosa. "Please! I will nurse him back to health!"

"I'm afraid that my son will have to be bribed. As you can see from this house, he has many expenses."

"I don't have anything but this lily on my face!" cried Rosa.

"That won't do," said the Sun's Mother. "But I have a plan. Don't worry!"

The Sun's Mother spun for Rosa a magnificent golden dress with long, wide sleeves to go with her golden veil from the Moon and her golden bracelets from the Wind.

"You must do exactly as I say," said the Sun's Mother. "At tonight's banquet, stuff as much bacon as you can find on the table up your sleeves."

"Bacon?" said Rosa.

"Bacon and grease," said the Sun's Mother.

"As much as possible—?"

"Up your sleeves," said the Sun's Mother, nodding.

At the banquet that night, Rosa was shocked to see her sisters, Isabel and Ana, sitting at the long table for the feast. Huge golden grapes hung from bowls on the table, and golden men and women plucked them and passed around platters of sun-cooked marvels.

"What are you doing here!" Rosa said, shaking beneath her golden veil and inside her golden dress. Her wicked sisters were dressed in drab cotton shifts from the Gold Hills Mall.

The other guests stopped dining and chatting to watch the sisters.

"Mother and Father told us also about the invisible doors in a day that a person can open to ride into another world," said Isabel sniffily. "We deserve to ride away on wings of joy, not you, Lily Face." And with that, she picked up a huge turkey leg and began to gnaw it.

"I will give up eating birds," said Ana, stuffing a huge pork chop into her face.

Rosa could feel her face burning as she did what the Sun's Mother commanded. She crammed bacon, fatty white bacon, thick slabs of greasy wet bacon, up her sleeves. There were so many trays of it!

Everyone was staring at her and choking with laughter.

"She's gone crazy!" announced Isabel.

But on the sly, she and Ana decided to imitate Rosa, for surely this must be some magic spell. They also stuffed bacon up their sleeves.

And where was the Sun? And the Sun's Mother?

A woman in golden velvet blew a trumpet and shouted, "Time for dancing! Everyone!"

Katherine Vaz

Out on the golden dance floor, as the music of the harps and cymbals, trumpets and organs, violins and tubas, harmonicas and guitars began their sunny tunes, Rosa forgot about everything but the golden, glorious sounds. She began to dance, hopping on one foot and the next, twirling about. She did a waltz and tango.

Her sisters did the same, jumping and shouting, flinging their arms into the air, not noticing that the bacon they had hidden up their sleeves was hurling up toward the ceiling and then falling onto the floor—SPLAT!—smearing the floor and making the other dancers slip and slide and trip.

SPLAT! SPLAT!

Bacon flung here and there! Bacon sticking to the bottoms of shoes! Dancers falling face-first into pork fat!

A golden woman screamed, "Are we in a frying pan?"

Rosa stopped dancing, because a miracle was happening. Out of her sleeves, diamonds were falling! She stared in shock. Diamonds, bright as chips of ice! The bacon that had been up her sleeves was turning into diamonds!

Isabel and Ana slipped and slid and were soon covered head to foot with bacon grease. A shout suddenly rang up to the domed ceiling:

"WHO IS RESPONSIBLE FOR THIS PIGSTY?"

The music stopped. The dancing stopped (except for the dancers who could not control their sliding about).

The Sun—like the largest torch imaginable—and

the Sun's Mother had entered the dining room. Isabel and Ana glanced up. They looked as if they were washerwomen down on their hands and knees, scrubbing the floor with bacon.

The Sun was so furious to see his golden floor so greasy that he threw open the main doors and tipped his palace so that the grease-covered people slid out, screeching like barnyard animals. They were tossed out into the empty sky.

Out went the twig-sisters, too.

Rosa's diamonds saved her from sliding away. They made a rough carpet that caught her feet and kept her in place. She stood braced up on the jewels and looked as best she could into the Sun's harsh stare. The Sun stopped tipping the palace, scooped up the diamonds, and said in heated words to Rosa, "What wish would you like me to grant?"

"I would like to nurse the hummingbird in your tower back to health," she said.

"Please try," said the Sun. "The sun is supposed to cheer creatures, but I have failed with him! Intolerable, I tell you!"

"Now, now, dear," said the Sun's Mother. "Calm down."

Rosa flew to the tower.

The hummingbird lay on a bed, bleeding from many wounds. His thin beak had been partly snapped off, and Rosa removed her golden bracelet to prop up his broken wing.

Katherine Vaz

The bird said, in pain, "Have you come to say good-bye?"

"I won't leave you," said Rosa, weeping. "I love you more than all the gold that was ever in Gold Hills, more than the gold in the Sun's palace. I love you more than all the water that bathes every sea creature. I give you the lily on my face so that you may drink of my sweetness."

Saying this, she turned the lily on her face, red as the red of the bird's wounds, toward him.

He was so overcome by her love that his gaze melted into the lily and into her, and when she glanced at him, her tears melted right on her eyes. He wept with gratitude, and she wept with worry, and soon they sailed out of the tower on the salty river they cried together.

The salty river made by their tears was vast enough to pour from the Sun's tower all the way back to Gold Hills.

And salt cures wounds.

The hummingbird healed, and Rosa was changed into a lily, because it was the best, magical part of her. She took root as a lily in a garden outside Gold Hills.

Every day, many times a day, the hummingbird kissed her. Because, after all, in Portuguese the word for "hummingbird" is *beija-flor*, which means "kiss-flower."

Rosa-the-Lily was so happy, and so was her hummingbird, that a golden glow remained around them. Because of this, the ghosts of the gold miners came out looking. They discovered Rosa-the-Lily and the hummingbird and told them their tall frontier tales. She told them that she'd been in a palace all of gold, but it blinded her. She preferred to live on Earth, where she did not have to blink and squint.

The hydrangeas planted nearby began to babble their own stories . . . and that is how Rosa learned that she'd joined the garden where her parents, Mother and Father, now lived as water-flowers.

As for Isabel and Ana, they were slippery with bacon grease as they fell from the sky, but they could not stop the stars from cutting them into little pieces. Each piece of the chopped-up sisters turned into a mosquito, like a tiny, buzzing, red devil.

Melting glances do not work to get rid of them, so go ahead and swat mosquitoes if you see them.

Glance deeply at lilies and into water, and you will feel a strange happiness. Your heart will beat like a hummingbird's. You will want to melt into the bright water that you see full of lilies; you will want to sink toward the roots and stories hidden in the earth.

(From the Portuguese legends "A Paraboinha de Oiro" and "A Cara de Boi," with much refiguring and many additions.)

Katherine Vaz

Katherine Vaz writes, "I have read straight through all of the *Oz* books in my mother's collection, and I'm still a huge fan of the *Babar* series. "The Kingdom of Melting Glances" borrows elements from two Portuguese folktales that feature bacon fat, princes as birds, and razor blades. I was going to leave out the razor blades, but my ten-year-old nephew, Daniel Duarte, my official consultant for the story in this collection, assured me that they made the bad sisters thrillingly more evil. So the razor blades are back in!"

Vaz is a writer and academic who teaches literature at the University of California at Davis. She is the author of two novels and the short story collection *Fado*, which won the Drue Heinz Literature Prize. Her writing often draws upon her Portugese-American background. She lives in Davis, California.

Hansel's Eyes

by Garth Nix

Hansel was ten and his sister, Gretel, was eleven when their stepmother decided to get rid of them. They didn't catch on at first, because the Hagmom (their secret name for her) had always hated them. So leaving them behind at the supermarket or forgetting to pick them up after school was no big deal.

It was only when their father got in on the "disappearing the kids" act that they realized it was serious. Although he was a weak man, they thought he might still love them enough to stand up to the Hagmom.

They realized he didn't the day he took them out into the woods. Hansel wanted to do the whole Boy Scout thing and take a water bottle and a pile of other stuff, but their dad said they wouldn't need it. It'd only be a short walk.

Then he dumped them. They'd just gotten out of the car when he took off. They didn't try to chase him. They knew the signs. The Hagmom had hypnotized him again or whatever she did to make him do things.

"Guess she's going to get a nasty surprise when we get back," said Hansel, taking out the map he'd stuffed down the front of his shirt. Gretel silently handed him the compass she'd tucked into her sock.

It took them three hours to get home, first walking, then in a highway patrol cruiser, and finally in their dad's car. They were almost back when the Hagmom rang on the cell phone. Hansel and Gretel could hear her screaming. But when they finally got home, she smiled and kissed the air near their cheeks.

"She's planning something," said Gretel. "Something bad."

Hansel agreed, and they both slept in their clothes, with some maps, the compass, and candy bars stuffed down their shirts.

Gretel dreamed a terrible dream. She saw the Hagmom creep into their room, quiet as a cat in her velvet slippers. She had a big yellow sponge in her hand, a sponge that smelled sweet, but too sweet to be anything but awful. She went to Hansel's bunk and pushed the sponge against his nose and face. His arms and legs thrashed for a second, then he fell back like he was dead.

Gretel tried and tried to wake from the dream, but when she finally opened her eyes, there was the yellow sponge and the Hagmom's smiling face and then the dream was gone and there was nothing but total, absolute darkness.

When Gretel did wake up, she wasn't at home. She was lying in an alley. Her head hurt, and she could hardly open her eyes because the sun seemed too bright.

"Chloroform," whispered Hansel. "The Hagmom drugged us and got Dad to dump us."

"I feel sick," said Gretel. She forced herself to stand and noticed that there was nothing tucked into her shirt, or Hansel's, either. The candy bars and the compass were gone.

"This looks bad," said Hansel, shielding his eyes with his hand and taking in the piles of trash, the broken windows, and the lingering, charcoal smell of past fires. "We're in the old part of the city, that got fenced off after the riots."

"She must hope someone will kill us," said Gretel. She scowled and picked up a jagged piece of glass, winding an old rag around it so she could use it like a knife.

"Probably," agreed Hansel, who wasn't fooled. He knew Gretel was scared, and so was he.

"Let's look around," Gretel said. Doing something would be better than just standing still, letting the fear grow inside them.

They walked in silence, much closer together than usual, their elbows almost bumping. The alley opened into a wide street that wasn't any better. The only sign of life was a flock of pigeons.

But around the next corner, Hansel backed up so

suddenly that Gretel's glass knife almost went into his side. She was so upset, she threw it away. The sound of shattering glass echoed through the empty streets and sent the pigeons flying.

"I almost stabbed you, you moron!" exclaimed Gretel. "Why did you stop?"

"There's a shop," said Hansel. "A brand-new one."

"Let me see," said Gretel. She looked around the corner for a long time, till Hansel got impatient and tugged at her collar, cutting off her breath.

"It is a shop," she said. "A Sony PlayStation shop. That's what's in the windows. Lots of games."

"Weird," said Hansel. "I mean, there's nothing here. No one to buy anything."

Gretel frowned. Somehow the shop frightened her, but the more she tried not to think of that, the more scared she got.

"Maybe it got left by accident," added Hansel. "You know, when they just fenced the whole area off after the fires."

"Maybe . . . ," said Gretel.

"Let's check it out," said Hansel. He could sense Gretel's uneasiness, but to him the shop seemed like a good sign.

"I don't want to," said Gretel, shaking her head.

"Well, I'm going," said Hansel. After he'd gone six or seven steps, Gretel caught up with him. Hansel smiled to himself. Gretel could never stay behind.

The shop was strange. The windows were so clear that you could see right inside, to the rows of PlayStations all set up ready to go, connected to really big television screens. There was even a Coke machine and a snack machine at the back.

Hansel touched the door with one finger, a bit hesitantly. Half of him wanted it to be locked, and half of him wanted it to give a little under his hand. But it did more than that. It slid open automatically, and a cool breeze of air-conditioned air blew across his face.

He stepped inside. Gretel reluctantly followed. The door shut behind them, and instantly all the screens came on and were running games. Then the Coke machine clunked out a couple of cans of Coke, and the snack machine whirred and hummed and a whole bunch of candy bars and chocolate piled up out the slot.

"Excellent!" exclaimed Hansel happily, and he went over and picked up a Coke. Gretel put out her hand to stop him, but it was too late.

"Hansel, I don't like this," said Gretel, moving back to the door. There was something strange about all this—the flicker of the television screens reaching out to her, beckoning her to play, trying to draw them both in . . .

Hansel ignored her, as if she had ceased to exist. He swigged from the can and started playing a game. Gretel ran over and tugged at his arm, but his eyes never left the screen.

Garth Nix

"Hansel!" Gretel screamed. "We have to get out of here!"

"Why?" asked a soft voice.

Gretel shivered. The voice sounded human enough, but it instantly gave her the mental picture of a spider, welcoming flies. Flies it meant to suck dry and hang like trophies in its web.

She turned around slowly, telling herself it couldn't really be a spider, trying to blank out the image of a hideous eight-legged, fat-bellied, fanged monstrosity.

When she saw it was only a woman, she didn't feel any better. A woman in her mid-forties, maybe, in a plain black dress, showing her bare arms. Long, sinewy arms that ended in narrow hands and long, grasping fingers. Gretel couldn't look directly at her face, just glimpsing bright red lipstick, a hungry mouth, and the darkest of sunglasses.

"So you don't want to play the games like your brother, Hansel," said the woman. "But you can feel their power, can't you, Gretel?"

Gretel couldn't move. Her whole body was filled up with fear because this woman was a spider, Gretel thought, a hunting spider in human shape, and she and Hansel were well and truly caught. Without thinking, she blurted out, "Spider!"

"A spider?" laughed the woman, her red mouth spreading wide, lips peeling back to reveal nicotine-stained teeth. "I'm not a spider, Gretel. I'm a shadow against the moon, a dark shape in the night doorway, a catch-as-catch-can . . . witch!"

"A witch," whispered Gretel. "What are you going to do with us?"

"I'm going to give you a choice that I have never given before," whispered the witch. "You have some smattering of power, Gretel. You dream true, and strong enough that my machines cannot catch you in their dreaming. The seed of a witch lies in your heart, and I will tend it and make it grow. You will be my apprentice and learn the secrets of my power, the secrets of the night and the moon, of the twilight and the dawn. Magic, Gretel, magic! Power and freedom and dominion over beasts and men!

"Or you can take the other path," she continued, leaning in close till her breath washed into Gretel's nose, foul breath that smelled of cigarettes and whisky. "The path that ends in the end of Gretel. Pulled apart for your heart, and lungs and liver and kidneys. Transplant organs are so in demand, particularly for sick little children with very rich parents! Strange, they never ask me where the organs come from."

"And Hansel?" whispered Gretel, without thinking of her own danger, or the seed in her heart that begged to be made a witch. "What about Hansel?"

"Ah, Hansel," cried the witch. She clicked her fingers, and Hansel walked over to them like a zombie, his fingers still twitching from the game.

"I have a particular plan for Hansel," crooned the witch. "Hansel with the beautiful, beautiful blue eyes."

She tilted Hansel's head back so his eyes caught the light, glimmering blue. Then she took off her sunglasses, and Gretel saw that the witch's own eyes were shriveled like raisins and thick with fat white lines like webs.

"Hansel's eyes go to a very special customer," whispered the witch. "And the rest of him? That depends on Gretel. If she's a good apprentice, the boy shall live. Better blind than dead, don't you think?" She snapped out her arm on the last word and grabbed Gretel, stopping her movement toward the door.

"You can't go without my leave, Gretel," said the witch. "Not when there's so much still for you to see. Ah, to see again, all crisp and clean, with eyes so blue and bright. Lazarus!"

An animal padded out from the rear of the shop and came up to the witch's hand. It was a cat, of sorts. It stood almost to the witch's waist, and it was multicolored, and terribly scarred, lines of bare skin running between patches of different-colored fur like a horrible jigsaw. Even its ears were different colors, and its tail seemed to be made of seven quite distinct rings of fur. Gretel felt sick as she realized it was a patchwork beast, sewn together from many different cats, and given life by the witch's magic.

Then Gretel noticed that whenever the witch turned her head, so did Lazarus. If she looked up, the cat looked up. If she turned her head left, it turned left. Clearly, the witch saw the world through the cat's eyes.

With the cat at her side, the witch pushed Gretel ahead of her, and whistled for Hansel to follow. They went through the back of the shop, then down a long stairway, deep into the earth. At the bottom, the witch unlocked the door with a key of polished bone.

Beyond the door was a huge cave, ill lit by seven soot-darkened lanterns. One side of the cave was lined with empty cages, each just big enough to house a standing child.

There was also an industrial cold room—a shed-sized refrigerator that had a row of toothy icicles hanging from the gutters of its sloping roof—that dominated the other side of the cave. Next to the cold room was a slab of marble that served as a table. Behind it, hanging from hooks in the damp stone of the cave wall, were a dozen knives and cruel-looking instruments of steel.

"Into the cage, young Hansel," commanded the witch, and Hansel did as he was told, without a word. The patchwork cat slunk after him, and shot the bolt home with a slap of its paw.

"Now, Gretel," said the witch. "Will you become a witch or be broken into bits?"

Gretel looked at Hansel in his cage, and then at the marble slab and the knives. There seemed to be no choice. At least if she chose the path of witchery, Hansel would only . . . only . . . lose his eyes. And perhaps they

Garth Nix

would get a chance to escape. "I will learn to be a witch," she said finally. "If you promise to take no more of Hansel than his eyes."

The witch laughed and took Gretel's hands in a bony grip, ignoring the girl's shudder. Then she started to dance, swinging Gretel around and around, with Lazarus leaping and screeching between them.

As she danced, the witch sang:

> "Gretel's chosen the witch's way,
> And Hansel will be the one to pay.
> Sister sees more and brother less
> Hansel and Gretel, what a mess!

Then she suddenly stopped and let go. Gretel spun across the cave and crashed into the door of one of the cages.

"You'll live down here," said the witch. "There's food in the cold room, and a bathroom in the last cage. I will instruct you on your duties each morning. If you try to escape, you will be punished."

Gretel nodded, but she couldn't help looking across at the knives sparkling on the wall. The witch and Lazarus looked, too, and the witch laughed again. "No steel can cut me, or rod mark my back," she said. "But if you wish to test that, it is Hansel I will punish."

Then the witch left, with Lazarus padding alongside her.

Gretel immediately went to Hansel, but he was still in the grip of the Playstation spell, eyes and fingers locked in some phantom game.

Next she tried the door, but sparks flew up and burned her when she stuck a knife in the lock. The door to the cold room opened easily enough, though, frosted air and bright fluorescent light spilling out. It was much colder inside than a normal refrigerator. One side of the room was stacked high with chiller boxes, each labeled with a red cross and a bright sticker that said, URGENT: HUMAN TRANSPLANT. Gretel tried not to look at them, or think about what they contained. The other side was stacked with all kinds of frozen food. Gretel took some spinach. She hated it, but spinach was the most opposite food to meat she could imagine. She didn't even want to think about eating meat.

The next day marked the first of many in the cave. The witch gave Gretel chores to do, mostly cleaning or packing up boxes from the cold room in special messenger bags the witch brought down. Then the witch would teach Gretel magic, like the spell that would keep herself and Hansel warm.

Always, Gretel lived with the fear that the witch would choose that day to bring down another child to be cut up on the marble slab, or to take Hansel's eyes. But the witch always came alone, and merely looked at Hansel through Lazarus's eyes and muttered, "Not ready."

So Gretel worked and learned, fed Hansel and

whispered to him. She constantly told him not to get better, to pretend that he was still under the spell. Either Hansel listened and pretended, even to her, or he really was still entranced.

Days went by, then weeks, and Gretel realized that she enjoyed learning magic too much. She looked forward to her lessons, and sometimes she would forget about Hansel for hours, forget that he would soon lose his eyes.

When she realized that she might forget Hansel all together, Gretel decided that she had to kill the witch. She told Hansel that night, whispering her fears to him and trying to think of a plan. But nothing came to her, for now Gretel had learned enough to know the witch really couldn't be cut by metal, or struck down by a blow.

The next morning, Hansel spoke in his sleep while the witch was in the cave. Gretel cried out from where she was scrubbing the floor, to try and cover it up, but it was too late. The witch came over and glared through the bars.

"So you've been shamming," she said. "But now I shall take your left eye, for the spell to graft it to my own socket must be fueled by your fear. And your sister will help me."

"No, I won't!" cried Gretel. But the witch just laughed and blew on Gretel's chest. The breath sank into her heart, and the ember of witchcraft that was there blazed up and grew, spreading through her body. Higher and higher it rose, till Gretel grew small inside her own head and could feel herself move around only at the witch's whim.

Then the witch took Hansel from the cage and bound him with red rope. She laid him on the marble slab, and Lazarus jumped up so she could see. Gretel brought her herbs, and the wand of ivory, the wand of jet, and the wand of horn. Finally, the witch chanted her spell. Gretel's mind went away completely then. When she came back to herself, Hansel was in his cage, one eye bandaged with a thick pad of cobwebs. He looked at Gretel through his other, tear-filled eye.

"She's going to take the other one tomorrow," he whispered.

"No," said Gretel, sobbing. "No."

"I know it isn't really you helping her," said Hansel. "But what can you do?"

"I don't know," said Gretel. "We have to kill her— but she'll punish you if we try and we fail."

"I wish it was a dream," said Hansel. "Dreams end, and you wake up. But I'm not asleep, am I? It's too cold, and my eye . . . it hurts."

Gretel opened the cage to hug him and cast the spell that would warm them. But she was thinking about cold—and the witch. "If we could trap the witch and Lazarus in the cold room somehow, they might freeze to death," she said slowly. "But we'd have to make it much colder, so she won't have time to cast a spell."

They went to look at the cold room, and found that it was set as cold as it would go. But Hansel found a barrel of liquid nitrogen at the back, and that gave him an idea.

120   Garth Nix

An hour later, they'd rigged their instant witch-freezing trap. Using one of the knives, Hansel unscrewed the inside handle of the door so there was no way to get out. Then they balanced the barrel on top of a pile of boxes, just past the door. Finally, they poured water everywhere to completely ice up the floor.

Then they took turns sleeping, till Gretel heard the click of the witch's key in the door. She sprang up and went to the cold room. Leaving the door ajar, she carefully stood on the ice and took the lid off the liquid nitrogen. Then she stepped back outside, pinching her nose and gasping. "Something's wrong, Mistress!" she exclaimed. "Everything's gone rotten."

"What!" cried the witch, dashing across the cave, her one blue eye glittering. Lazarus ran at her heels from habit, though she no longer needed his sight.

Gretel stood aside as she ran past, then gave her a hefty push. The witch skidded on the ice, crashed into the boxes, and fell flat on her back just as the barrel toppled over. An instant later, her final scream was smothered in a cloud of freezing vapor.

But, Lazarus, quicker than any normal cat, did a backflip in midair, even as Gretel slammed the door. Ancient stitches gave way, and the cat started coming apart, accompanied by an explosion of the magical silver dust that filled it and gave it life.

Gretel relaxed for an instant as the dust obscured the beast, then screamed as the front part of Lazarus jumped out at her, teeth snapping. She kicked at it, but the cat was too swift, its great jaws meeting around her ankle. Gretel screamed again, and then Hansel was there, shaking the strange dust out of the broken body as if he were emptying a vacuum cleaner. In a few seconds there was nothing left of Lazarus but its head and an empty skin. Even then it wouldn't let go, till Hansel forced its mouth open with a broomstick and pushed the snarling remnant across the floor and into one of the cages.

Gretel hopped across and watched it biting the bars, its green eyes still filled with magical life and hatred. "Hansel," she said. "Your own eye is frozen with the witch. But I think I can remember the spell—and there is an eye for the taking here."

So it was that when they entered the cold room later to take the key of bone from the frozen, twisted body of the witch, Hansel saw the world through one eye of blue and one of green.

Later, when they found their way home, it was the sight of that green eye that gave the Hagmom a heart attack and made her die. But their father was still a weak man, and within a year he thought to marry another woman who had no love for his children. Only this time, the new Hagmom faced a Gretel who was more than half a witch, and a Hansel who had gained strange powers from his magic cat's-eye.

But that is all another story. . . .

Garth Nix is the author of the children's fantasy novel *The Ragwitch*, and two novels for an older audience, *Sabriel* and *Shade's Children*. He first encountered Grimms' fairy tales when they were read to him at the age of five or six. He spent the next two years attempting to spin straw into gold, turn pumpkins into carriages, and find a bearskin to put on—all without success. He chose Hansel and Gretel for retelling, as it was always a favorite, probably because his mother made him a fantastic gingerbread house for his eighth birthday, complete with a witch made out of sweets. He chose to set the retold story in a city because he has always found being lost in cities much more terrifying than being lost in the woods—or, in his case, the bush of Australia. Garth lives in Sydney, but has been lost in many different countries.

Becoming Charise

by Kathe Koja

In the back of the school bus, hunched next to a window smeared and cloudy with breath, sketchbook open on her knees: Charise. Sitting alone; again; always. Imagining the world.

"Hey, Nerdstein," Tibb Gleason said, shoving her shoulder, ruining her pencil's line. "Draw a picture of this."

Charise bit her lip, erased the mark, started drawing again. Not the world around her, the world as it was, but her world, the way she imagined things could be. A world where no one hurt animals, or polluted the water and skies. A world where no one hurt anyone, where no one called names, where girls could wear oversized red sweatshirts printed with pictures of Albert Einstein and not get called a nerd. Or a geek. Or worse. All the time.

Charise wondered if Einstein had ever been called a nerd.

She had read everything she could find about Albert Einstein: how he had decided, at age twelve, to solve the riddle of the "huge world" all around him. How he was such a crappy student, he left school at fifteen. How four papers he wrote, scientific papers, did more to solve that riddle than anyone before or since. Charise thought he might be a kind of saint, a saint of knowing, if there was such a thing. Charise loved knowing things, how things worked, what they did; she knew that Knowing was the first step to Becoming.

"I want to Become," she told her Aunt Tamara. Breakfast, the windows dark around them; raisin bagels and orange juice fluorescent in her glass. Beneath the chair, her mutt terrier, Dino, waited for the usual crumbs.

Aunt Tamara poured herself some orange juice, sliced a bagel with one swift swipe. "Become what? You could be an artist, with all that drawing you do. Or maybe a scientist. Or an engineer—"

"I don't mean that," Charise said. "I mean . . . I just want to Become." Become what I am, she wanted to say, but didn't know how. Like a caterpillar is a butterfly, somewhere inside its genes; like an atom splits. Like a piece of paper and a Number Two pencil are a drawing, when they meet a particular hand and eye, when all of it finally gets together, to Become what it somehow was, all along, forever . . . Aunt Tamara was smiling at her.

"You want another bagel?"

Dino put up his pointy little ears; Charise shook her head. "I gotta go."

"I'll see you after work," Aunt Tamara said.

On the bus, Charise had to squeeze past some seventh graders, big girls in bright parkas, pink and green. In seventh grade they did a science unit on Einstein; that was something to wait for, a bright marker on the dull road of the days. Maybe it would be different if she were somewhere else, a different road, but Jackson was a school like a cheese sandwich was a meal; it would get you by, but that was all. Not a hot pepperoni pizza, like, say, the Bayley Academy. Charise had heard about Bayley: A couple kids from Jackson—smart kids; lucky kids—had gone there. It lived in her mind like a moon, bright and unreachable, something to consider at night.

But today was orange juice and bagels and the bus, the jostling halls of Jackson, trying not to mind that she had no locker partner, trying to get through the day.

It had always been hard for Charise to fit in. Too wild for the smart kids, too smart for the wild kids, as if school were one kind of puzzle, and she was a piece from another box. Don't you want to go out and play? Aunt Tamara used to ask her as she sat with cookies or a Coke, legs hooked around the kitchen chair, Dino alert beneath. Or maybe ask a friend over?

I don't have any friends, she said in her head, but to Aunt Tamara she would say, "Not today," or, "Not right now." In grade school most of the kids had seemed silly, babyish, but, still, it hurt to stand and watch as they played soccer or four-square, or walked home together after school. She kept hoping that one day things might be different—"You wait," Aunt Tamara kept telling her, "things will change for you, you'll see"—but, still, they were the same. And the hurt was the same, a dark, dry ache not in her center but deeper, as if she were a kind of funnel, and the emptiness before the bottom was part of the hurting, too.

I'm just different, Charise told herself, biting her lip. I bet Einstein was different, too.

At Jackson there were three groups of kids. The largest was the Regulars, the middle-of-the-roaders, who moved past Charise in the stream of the hall like boats around a buoy, avoiding her without effort, without even seeing she was there. In the lunchroom, hunched over her sketchbook at the end of the unpopular kids' table, where Clarissa and DeeDee and DeJuan played their endless games of Hearts or Bump Rummy, she sometimes heard, "Hey, Geekstein!" from one of the Regulars, calling out to make the others laugh: mean, but not too mean, the way they might use a magnifying glass to burn up ants on the sidewalk, never thinking it might hurt the ants to be killed.

But the kids who did think, the smart kids, were always busy with stuff like student council, or the school newspaper, or the debate group, things Charise didn't want to do. And, anyway, they didn't want to hang out with her, either; they respected her for her brains, but that was all. Respect is different from being friends: You can respect someone you don't even like.

And the third group, the outsiders, the wild kids like Tibb Gleason—they always sat in the back, sniggering to each other and writing swear words in their books, or on the desks for other kids to find later. They ignored Charise unless they needed a quiz answer, then called her a bitch if she wouldn't give it to them.

Which she wouldn't. "You want to know the answer?" she would whisper, very low, so her lips barely moved and the teacher couldn't see. "Then study." Why should they sponge off her hard work? Every night she took home books, she went to the library, she went on the Net on her Aunt Tamara's computer: "What are you doing?" Aunt Tamara would call from the living room, where she sat with her own books, her night school work. "Are you online?"

"I'm downloading some stuff," Charise would call back. "For school." Mostly it wasn't for school, it was for herself, things she wanted to know about, but Aunt Tamara didn't mind. She said learning was learning. Mr. Mahfouz said the same thing.

Mr. Mahfouz was the sixth-grade science teacher. Some kids called him Mr. MahFool, but most of the kids liked him: He told jokes, he brought in laser games and giant Slinkys, he didn't care if you laughed or shouted out. Sometimes he wore funny T-shirts under his sport coat, or a baseball cap with a cardinal on it, for some sports team he liked. All sports were a closed book to Charise, but Mr. Mahfouz talked about the physics of baseball; he could find science in anything. Even TV.

"Your mission," he told the class that day, "is to find science on TV. Or in a TV: Cut it up, dissect it, see what you get. And then tell me all about it in a report. No less than five pages, at least three illustrations. That means pictures, guys."

Most of the kids watched nature shows; a few rented videos and brought them in. Mark Carver, who was editor of the school paper, did a newspaper story, with three photographs, of him and his friends "dissecting" a TV with a screwdriver. Charise did her report on the science of TV—what made it work, why you saw a picture when you clicked the remote. "This is dynamite," Mr. Mahfouz said, and put up her report in the showcase at the front of the room. "Charise, come see me after class."

"Dynamite you, Geekstein," said Tibb Gleason when Charise sat down again.

When the day was over, she came back to Mr. Mahfouz, who sat behind his desk, sorting papers. Lockers click-and-banging, a faraway shout in the hall; the school grew quiet as she waited. Finally, Mr. Mahfouz said "Finished," setting the papers aside. "Sorry it took so long. . . . You know, your report was really excellent, Charise. Even for you."

Charise nodded, watchful. She knew more was coming.

"Do you like it here, at Jackson?" Did she like it? What kind of a question was that? "Reason I ask," he said, "is there's a couple of placements opening up at Bayley—the Bayley Academy, ever heard of it?—and I'd like to sponsor you for one of them." From the papers on his desk he chose two, along with a brochure, slick and glossy like a magazine. "Take that home, let your folks have a look at it and, if you're interested, we'll talk some more."

THE BAYLEY ACADEMY OF ARTS & SCIENCE: slim black letters on a cool blue background, lots of stuff about academic excellence, a world of learning. And lots of pictures: of kids in a laboratory, kids on a stage, kids with computers; lots of computers. This was no cheese sandwich. It was a big, juicy pizza with everything, the kind of place Einstein would have loved.

Charise kept the brochure hidden in her backpack, as if it might be taken from her, or vanish like a magic trick; she read it like the Bible, she read it for a week, looking at the kids, the labs, the computers—

"I'd like to sponsor you . . ."

no more Tibb Gleason, no more Geckstein

a world of learning

Aunt Tamara you have to say yes

—until at last, at Friday dinner, trying her best to sound casual: "From Mr. Mahfouz," Charise said, sliding the brochure across the table. "He said to show it to you; he said he'd sponsor me if I wanted."

130   Kathe Koja

Fork in hand but she could not eat, could not swallow, could barely breathe as she watched Aunt Tamara read the whole thing, even the papers inside. Dino shuffled beneath her chair; the dinner grew cold. Finally, Aunt Tamara looked up, without a smile. "Honey," she said, in a voice like lead, "smart as you are, I don't know if this is the place for you. The kids would be—very different from what you're used to."

Charise felt her heart beating, a hard, red drum: like an atom, splitting. Her mouth was open, but Aunt Tamara was still talking. "—way across town, there's no school bus to get you there, and I have to be at work by—"

From inside the drum, the atom, her voice dry and far away: "I could ride my bike."

"It's across town, Charise. And what about wintertime?"

"I could, I could take a regular bus, I could walk—" but Aunt Tamara was shaking her head, she was closing the brochure, she was saying, "Charise, honey, I'm sorry," but Charise was already gone, away, slamming her bedroom door, crouching on the floor with her arms clenched around her body till she was dark and hard and small; like a rock: like a seed. She was crying, but she didn't know it.

I want to Become. I want to Become.

She would ride her bike, take a bus, walk if she had to, walk every mile there and back. She would go to Bayley, she would become Einstein, she would—

"Charise?"

Hard and dark: her arms were cramping: her legs had fallen asleep. Aunt Tamara's knock was as gentle as her voice: "Charise, please, open the door."

"No," she said, but now she knew she was crying, felt the tears like lines on her face, felt their salt and cloudy heat; their elements, Mr. Mahfouz would say. She cried until she thought she was empty, then cried a little more. The door nudged open a crack: Dino, come to lie beside her in the darkness. She was still crying when at last she fell asleep.

"Your aunt called me," said Mr. Mahfouz as soon as Charise walked into class; he looked sad. "Can you stop in after school for a minute?"

"Sure." No tears today, Charise kept her face still, kept her hands in her pockets as Mr. Mahfouz talked: Your aunt said, so and so and so on, watching her face as he spoke. "I have to tell you," he said at last, slumping a little in his rolling chair, "I'm pretty disappointed. What about you?" His face looked tired, like a helium balloon the day after the party, as if something good had gone out of him.

"Yeah," Charise said, "I am." She shrugged a little, a thin motion. "So what."

"So I guess we'll have to do the best we can, you and me." Mr. Mahfouz sighed. "You know the story of the ugly duckling?"

Kathe Koja

She nodded, sharp, almost rude with the weight of her heart inside her. All she wanted now was for him to stop talking so she could get away, get her coat, get out of this crappy school for today, at least . . . but Mr. Mahfouz was waiting for an answer, so, "Yeah," she said, looking not at him but out the window, into the gray slant of afternoon sun. "He grew up to be a swan, or something. So what."

"So he never was a duckling in the first place," Mr. Mahfouz said. His voice was calm now, and very precise, the way it was when he was explaining something, something he expected them to get. Her to get. "He was going to become a swan. No matter where he went, no matter what he did—it was in his genes, Charise, you understand what I'm saying?"

"I understand," she said, still wanting to get away, wishing she was in her room, wishing she could find Einstein and tell him her problems, tell him how much she wished she could

become

what she was meant to be, what she was inside—

a swan.

Like a pencil and some paper is a picture; like a caterpillar is a butterfly. Like she was what she was, Charise, part of a puzzle that was not the puzzle she knew, but still part of something bigger: a different puzzle, somewhere else. Maybe at Bayley, or maybe not. Did it matter? In the end, it probably didn't matter.

It was in his genes, Charise, you understand what I'm saying?

"Charise?" said Mr. Mahfouz, leaning forward, arms on the desk, and, "Yes," she said, because she got it now, she knew why he was smiling; she was smiling, too. Not a big smile but a bright one, like a little moon a million miles away, getting bigger as you get closer to it, and, "You know," said Mr. Mahfouz, "you can always try again next year. For Bayley, I mean. Your aunt might—"

"Einstein dropped out of school," Charise said. Now her smile was a grin.

Mr. Mahfouz laughed. "You don't have to do everything Einstein did," he said.

On the bus, Tibb Gleason stuck his foot out in the aisle, but Charise stepped over it as if it wasn't there; quack, quack, she thought. Quack you, Tibb Gleason. Plopping down into the seat, she took out her sketchbook and spent the ride home drawing: The world she wanted, Einstein's "huge world," and herself, grown up, in the middle, with big white wings like a swan's.

Kathe Koja

Kathe Koja says: "I chose to retell this story because I have been the Ugly Duckling more than once: I know how it hurts, and I know that you have to be who you are, no matter what. I hope this story helps another duckling, somewhere else."

Koja is the author of several adult novels, including *The Cipher*, which was cowinner of the Bram Stoker Award for Superior Achievement in a First Novel; *Skin*; and *Strange Angels*. She lives in Michigan with her husband, artist Rick Lieder, and her son, Aaron.

The Seven Stage a Comeback

by Gregory Maguire

1. So that's how it is, fellows.
   The man with the crazed expression
   Clawed open her coffin,
   Kissed her awake,
   And carried her off.
   There goes our lovely daughter.
   All we have left of her
   Is the apple that tumbled from her lips
   And the glass box we nested her in.

2. We're better off without her.
   I always told you that.
   And you, and you, and you two, too.
   (*You*, I rarely spoke to. Mop up your nose.)
   Wasn't she always on us about something?

"Can't you tidy the woodpile some?"
"Hasn't anyone ever heard of a thing called soap?"
"I don't trust little men with beards."
And then with the sighs.
The expressive eyes.
Followed by floods of agitated song.
Frankly, when she ate that poisoned apple—
Oh, yes, I was sad, I cried—
But you want to know what else?
I thought: *At last. A little peace and quiet around here.*

3. So why are your eyes all rimmed with red?
   You loved her as we all did.
   Her with her lips like October apples,
   Her hair like the wind on April nights.
   Or did you just like having someone to complain
   about?
   You kept your vigil as I did. As we all did.

4. And all that's left is the apple and the coffin.
   The fruit and the glass.
   And our troubled hearts.
   Let's worry a solution out of this.
   What could we do?
   Put the bit of the apple in the glass coffin
   And close it up again?
   The coffin keeps things pretty fresh.
   And for a good, long time, too, it seems.
   You never know when we'll need a bit of poison
   apple again.

5. Let's take the coffin on our backs
    And wander o'er the mountain tracks.
    Sing ho! for the life of a dwarf.

6. This isn't the time for singing.
    But it's not a bad idea.
    I say let's muscle it out. Come on.
    Let's get this baby home.
    All together now, on a count of three—
    One, two—alley-oop and upsy-daisy.
    You, carry the iron-head hammer.
    Mind how you swing it, dolt.
    And stop with that racket.

7. Ohhhhhhh, ohhhhhhh, ohhhhhhh, ohhhhhhh,
    ohhhhhhh, ohhhhhhh, ohhhhhhh.

1. So listen, guys. Put down your beer steins.
    Life hasn't been kind to us.
    We find an orphan girl, we take her in.
    Locate some moldy blankets to keep her warm.
    Porridge in the morning, porridge in the evening.
    A little dwarf folk music to cheer her up.
    It was a humble life, but it was ours,
    And freely we gave it to her.
    No wonder we're still upset.
    No wonder we can't focus.
    On our plates, our gray beard hardens.
    In the cold cauldron, our soup grows a skin of scum.

Gregory Maguire

We have to shape up. We're falling to pieces here.
2. Easy come, easy go.
    We're better off without her.
    Remember, I always said that.
3. You are the one who speaks with the sharpest tongue,
    But you're the one who moans her name in your
    sleep.
    Face it. We all miss her.
    When's the last time any one of us laughed out loud?
    Sorrow has a name, and its name is loneliness.
    Sorrow has a shape, and its shape is absence.
    Sorrow is a sickness like any other.
    We don't manage to do what we should.
    We never go out with our iron-head hammer
    To bash the jewels out of secret caves.
    Our hearts are bashed instead.
    But what can we do?
4. We could go find her where she is.
    We could beg her to come back.
    We could bring the glass coffin.
    We could lay her where she was.
5. Let's take the coffin on our backs
    And wander o'er the mountain tracks.
    Sing ho! for the life of a dwarf.
6. Please, would you stop your singing, please?
    It's hard to think.
    Though I'm not one for kidnapping old friends,
    She did leave us high and dry.

The Seven Stage a Comeback   139

She married that traveling prince.
They could be nine kingdoms away by now.
It has been months already.
I doubt we could ever find her.
But I'm a one for putting on boots
And marching impressively right off a cliff.
Better than sitting around with tears in our beards!
Let me hunt for a map, a compass.
We need cloaks, and staffs, and gumption.
Up from your sloth, you miserable slugs.
Pocket your bread and cork your ale.
Tighten your belts and lace your boots.
Somebody grab the iron-head hammer,
Somebody bring the silver guitar.
You, are you weeping again, you fool?

7. Ohhhhhh, ohhhhhh. Ohhhhhh, ohhhhhh. Ohhhhhh, ohhhhhh.

1. Good-bye to the house in the autumn woods.
   Good-bye to our hermit hideaway.
   There's no life left for us at home.
   This little house, this moldy tomb—
   Not our tomb, but the grave and marker
   Of what we lost when she went away.
   Now hoist the coffin on your backs,
   And off we go.
2. We're better off without her.

140   Gregory Maguire

We're better off without her.
We're better off without her.

3. So you say. So you keep saying.
   But you walk faster than the rest of us.
   Now the air is cold, the wind is high,
   The light is wet, the clouds come in.
   I feel a sadness in my bones.
   It never was to come to this.
   We took her in when she was lost,
   But then we lost her in our turn.
   And are we losing ourselves as well?

4. We'll find our beauty where she rests,
   And coax her home.
   What's wrong with that?
   The least she owes us is a little loyalty.
   She never should have eaten the apple, one,
   Nor, two, attracted the first available prince.
   Ours is not to harm or hurt her.
   Just to keep her safely with us.

5. We have the coffin on our backs
   And wander o'er the mountain tracks.
   Sing ho! for the life of a dwarf.

6. Keep the pace, steady she goes.
   If we suffer one turned ankle,
   One hurt shoulder, one slipped hip,
   Down goes the coffin, and crash goes the glass.
   Out goes the apple bit, bouncing away,
   Into the million brown leaves of the forest floor.

Lost as lost, now and forevermore.
And all our hopes will be lost as well.
You, are you weeping again, you fool?
7. Ohhhhh, ohhhhh. Ohhhhh, ohhhhh.
    Ohhhhh, ohhhhh.

1. The wind on the mountain chills my heart.
2. We're better off without her.
3. She's hoping we rescue her, I know.
4. I fear the clouds are seeded with snow.
5. Sing ho! for the life of a dwarf. Brr.
6. I'll smash your head with the iron-head hammer
    If you don't stop your infernal racket.
7. Ohhh. Ohhh. Ohhh. Ohhh.

1. Now here, a fallen tree. We'll cross
    This rushing icy mountain stream.
    Don't drop the coffin into the flood,
    For there it would sink, and clear as light,
    We'd search in vain and never see it.
    Steady your feet, and steady your hearts.
2. We're better off without her.
    But should we come across her . . .
    I'll be the one to ask her.
    How she could ever leave us.
    I'll laugh at any answer.

Gregory Maguire

We're better off without her.

3. We aren't her abductors.
   Just friend who come a-calling.
   We'll ask her to rejoin us.
   The coffin waits.

4. The coffin waits.

5. The coffin weighs upon our backs
   And makes too steep these snowy tracks.
   Sing ho! for the life of a dwarf.

6. I see the ice that prickles in the nose
   And crusts the corners of our jeweled eyes
   Invades the reaches of our dwarfish hearts.
   I fear what we're about.
   I cannot stop.
   We are bewitched; no more, no less.
   Her beauty calls us, and we can't escape.
   Let's save our breath in this bitter cold.
   Mind how you swing that hammer, clumsy oaf!

7. Ohh, ohh, ohh.

1. Here in the inn-yard, huddled about a fire,
   A tankard of watered beer, we take our rest,
   The winter months have brought us a hopeful spring.
   Today we learn that the girl we seek
   Lives just beyond the ridge, in a noble home.
   No dragons to guard the moat, no spells to break.

No soldiers lurking upon the shingled roofs.
Nothing to stop us from going the final steps.
Here we'll commit what crime we may,
And live to rue, or praise, the day.

7. Oh, oh, oh, oh, oh.

2. We're better off without her.
Let's give her the poisoned sleep
And lock her within her windows.
What's dead cannot live to leave us again.
We love her too much to allow her to live.

7. Oh, oh, oh, oh.

3. We're smaller than human men, with smaller hearts.
Our strength is in mighty arms, for smashing rocks,
Our strength is for swinging hammers with iron
heads.
We aren't built to know what's right or wrong.
We're hardly more than pagan animals.
We met her when she was young, we took her in,
As much to serve us at our filthy home
As out of any wish to do charity.
Let's finish the job we started, and shed no tears
For being smaller creatures than we'd like.
Up to the mansion, then, to take her back,
There to cherish her incorruptible corpse.

7. Oh, oh, oh.

4. The apple awaits to do its lethal job.
The glassy walls of the coffin are polished clear,
Its hinges oiled silent by dwarfish spit.

Gregory Maguire

Now we to our work, and she, our beauty—
She to her work, again, at last, forever.
7. Oh, oh.
5. Let's lift the coffin from our backs
And see what sleeper it attracts.
Sing ho! for the life of a dwarf.
7. Oh.
6. We're decided then; the deed is clear.
The time is now.
We leave to claim our prize.
7. ——

1. There she sits, in an orchard of apple trees.
Who could have thought she would be more beautiful
Than memory could picture?
2. We're better off without—we're better off—we're better—
3. You stutter out of shock, and so do I.
Hush, lest she hears us before we make our approach.
Her hair is longer, see how the wind enjoys it!
See how her smile blossoms; she looks aside,
Shyly, at mending collected inside the basket
That rests in the fragrant grass near her pretty feet.
4. She always loved the household task.
She sang when she worked.

Who can forget her voice?
But once I wondered, bringing the silver guitar,
If she sang to keep her spirits high.
As if we were not the world she truly wanted,
However good our porridge, sweet our music.
Now let us creep up closer to observe.

5. Sing ho, sing ho, sing ho.
   Off with the girl and away we go.

6. She smiles upon the laundry with radiant look,
   She stirs the cloth as if something lies gently within,
   A bruisable apple, a blossom, a porcelain toy.
   Now is the time. There is nobody else around.
   At the count of three, we leap from these thickets, see,
   Surround her—confound her—accuse her—
   reclaim her—
   One—two—

7. Three
   Is the number we never expected to see.
   Yes, you will listen, all of you! Hear me out.
   It is not just the prince and the princess we disturb.
   That basket of washing is laughing at its mother.
   There is a child within. Are you wholly blind?
   I'll swing this iron-head hammer at your skulls.
   I'll smash the coffin seven directions to heaven.
   Dwarfish mischief we make, and dwarfish music,
   But mischief and music never come closer together
   Than in the laugh of an infant adoring its mother.

Gregory Maguire

1. We come from distant regions, cold and wild,
   To bring you dwarfish music for your child.
2. We come to visit you, and we will try
   To sing the babe a pretty lullaby.
3. We come to see what loneliness is worth;
   It brings new life upon the ancient earth.
4. We smash the coffin of your former days
   Seeing the happiness that spills in your gaze.
5. No coffin is left to lift upon our backs
   And carry home along the mountain tracks.
   Sing ho! for the life of a dwarf.
6. Now standing in splintered glass, in scented grass,
   We sing you all our love, before we pass.
7. All of us loved her as much as we could grieve.
   As hard as we could do, each in our way.
   Now hand me the silver guitar, and I will play
   The final notes before we take our leave.

She thinks:

After this horrible winter, how sweet the air feels!

How silly I'm being. Fanciful, flighty! But I can't help it. It's almost as if the wind were strumming invisible harps.

And the light is a pretty thing today. Pinkish, rosy. It must be the sun streaming down through the apple blossoms.

Reminds me of a dream I must have had. As if I had

lived somewhere else, once upon a time. I never did, of course. I was always here, awake, and in my life. With my loved one just within the sound of my voice, and my baby here at my feet. Smiling as if at some mysterious joke. Smiling as if the happily ever after of stories begins right now, at the very start of life.

Gregory Maguire

Gregory Maguire has written twelve novels for children, including The Hamlet Chronicles: *Seven Spiders Spinning, Six Haunted Hairdos, Five Alien Elves*, and so on. His novels for adults include *Wicked: The Life and Times of the Wicked Witch of the West* and *Confessions of an Ugly Stepsister*. He writes, "When I was seven I came across the stories about Baba Yaga printed in the children's magazine called *Jack and Jill*. Twenty years later I published *The Dream Stealer*, a children's novel with Baba Yaga as a character. I've always liked the witches in fairy tales best—better than dragons or unicorns. But dwarves and trolls and the like are pretty cool, too, so that's what attracted me to Snow White. I've suspected for some time that I have a dwarf colony out behind the garage, but maybe it's moles." Maguire's typewriter, garage, and dwarves-or-moles are in Concord, Massachusetts.

The Twelve
Dancing Princesses

by Patricia A. McKillip

One day long ago in a faraway country, a young soldier, walking home from a battle he had fought for the king, found himself lost in a forest. The road he followed dwindled away, leaving him standing among silent trees, with the sun just setting at his back, and the moon just rising ahead of him. Caught alone and astray between night and day, he thought to himself, There are worse things that could be. He had seen many of them on the battlefield. He was alone because he had watched his best friend die; he had given his last few coins to another soldier trying to walk home with only one foot. But he himself, though worn and bloodied with battle, had kept all his bones, and his eyes, and he even had a little bread and cheese in his pack to eat. He settled himself into a tangle of tree roots, where he could watch the moon, and took out his simple meal. He had opened his mouth to take the first bite when a voice at his elbow said, "One bite is a feast to those who have nothing."

He turned, wondering who had crept up so noiselessly to sit beside him. It was a very old woman. Her bones bumped under the surface of her brown, sagging skin like the tree roots under the earth. Her pale eyes, which now held only a memory of the blue they had been, were fixed on the heel of bread, the rind of cheese in his hand. He sighed, for he was very hungry. But so must she be, scuttling like an animal among the trees, with no one to care for her. There are worse things, he thought, than having a little less of something.

So he said, tearing the bread and cheese apart and giving her half, "Then feast with me."

"You are kind, young soldier," she said in her high wavery voice, and bit into her scanty supper as if it might vanish before she could finish it. After she had swallowed her last bite and searched for crumbs, she spoke again. "What is your name?"

"Val," he answered.

"A good name for a soldier. Did you win the battle?"

Val shrugged. "So they say. I could not see, from where I stood, that winning was much better than losing."

"And now what will you do?"

"I don't know. My younger brother has married and

taken care of the family farm and our parents while I have been fighting. I will find my way back and show them that I'm still alive, and then find something to do in the world. After all, someone with nothing has nothing to lose."

"You have a fair and honest face," the old woman said. "That's something." Her pale eyes caught moonlight and glinted, so suddenly and strangely, that he started. "How would you like to be king?"

He swallowed a laugh along with a lump of bread. "Better than being a beggar."

"Then follow this road through the forest. It will take you into the next kingdom, where the king and queen there are desperate for help. They have twelve beautiful daughters—"

"Twelve!"

"None of them will marry; they will laugh at every suitor. The king locks them in their room every night; and every morning he finds them sleeping so soundly, they will not wake until noon, and at the foot of every bed, a pair of satin shoes so worn with dancing, they must be thrown away. But no one knows how the princesses get out of the room, or where they go to dance. The king has promised his kingdom and a daughter to any man who can solve this mystery."

"Any man," Val repeated, and felt a touch of wonder in his heart, where before there had been nothing. "Even me."

Patricia A. McKillip

"Even you. But you must be careful. The king is half mad with worry and fear for his daughters. He will kill any man who fails, even princes who might one day marry his daughters."

The young soldier pondered that. "Well," he said softly. "I have faced death before. No one ever offered to make me king if I survived." He stood up. "There's moon enough to see by, tonight. Where is the road to that kingdom?"

"Under your feet," she answered, and there it was, washed with light and winding among the trees. Val stared at the old woman; her face rippled into a thousand wrinkles as she smiled.

"Two things. One: Drink nothing that the princesses give you. And two"—she touched the dusty cloak at his back—"this will make you invisible when you follow them at night. It pays," she added, as he slid his pack strap over his shoulder, "to be kind to crones."

"So I hope," he breathed, and stepped onto the moonlit road, wondering if he would find death at its end, or love.

Death, he thought instantly, when he met the father of the twelve princesses. The king, wearing black velvet and silver mail, was tall and gaunt, with long, iron-gray hair and a lean, furrowed face. His eyes were black and terrible with frustration and despair. He wore a sword so long and heavy, it would have dragged on the ground at Val's side. He kept one hand always on it; Val wondered if he used it to slay the princes who failed him.

But he spoke to the young soldier with courtesy. Val found himself soaking in a fragrant bath while a barber cut his hair. Then he dressed in fine, elegant clothes, though he refused, for no reasons he gave, to part with his torn, dusty cloak. He sat down to a meal so wondrously cooked that he could scarcely name what he ate. When night fell, the king took him to the princesses' bedchamber.

The doors to the long chamber opened to such color, such rich wood and fabric, such movement of slender, jeweled hands and glowing hair, and bright, curious eyes, so many sweet, laughing voices, that Val froze on the threshold, mute with astonishment that any place so lovely and full of grace could exist in the world he knew. "My daughters," the king said as they floated toward him, breasting the air like swans in their lacy, flowing nightgowns. "The queen named them after flowers. Aster, Bluet, Columbine, Delphinium, Eglantine, Fleur, Gardenia, Heather, Iris, Jonquil, Lily, and Mignonette. She could not find an appropriate flower for K."

"Kumquat," one with long, golden hair giggled behind her hands.

"Knotweed," another said with an explosion of laughter into her nearest sister's shoulder. Then they were all silent, their eyes of amber, emerald, sapphire, unblinking and wide, watching Val like a circle of cats, he thought, watching a sparrow.

Patricia A. McKillip

He said, scarcely hearing himself, while his own eyes were charmed from face to face, "There are folk names for flowers, sometimes, that queens may not know. Kestrel's Eye, farmers call a kind of sunflower, for its smallness and the color of its center."

"Kestrel," a princess with a mass of dark, curly hair and golden eyes repeated. Her beauty held more dignity and assurance than her sisters'; her eyes, smiling at the handsome young stranger, seemed full of secrets. "A pretty word. You might have been Kestrel, then, Lily, and Mignonette would have been you, if our mother had known."

She was the oldest, Val guessed, and was proved right when the youngest protested, "But, Aster, I am Mignonette; I do not want to be Lily."

"Don't worry, goose, you may stay yourself." She yawned, then, and stepped forward to kiss their grim father. "How tired I am, suddenly! I could sleep for a month!"

"I wish you all would," the king murmured, bending as one by one they brushed his face with kisses. They only laughed at him and vanished behind the hangings of lace and gauze around their beds; they were as silent then as if they had already begun to dream.

The king showed Val a small room at the end of the bedchamber, where he could pretend to sleep as he waited for the princesses to reveal the mystery of their dancing. "Many men have come here," the king said, "seeking to win my kingdom, thinking it a trifling matter to outwit my daughters and take my crown. They are all dead, now, even the jesting, lighthearted princes. My daughters show no mercy, and neither do I. But if you fail, I will be sorry."

Val bowed his head. "So will I," he answered. "How strange it seems that yesterday I had nothing to lose, and today I have everything. Except love."

"That alone drives me mad," the king said harshly. "They can love no one. Nothing. They laugh at the young men I put to death. As if they are spellbound. . . ." He turned, begging rather than warning as he closed the door. "Do not fail."

Val sat down on the bed, which was the first he had seen in many months, and the last he dared sleep in. He had just pulled off his boots when the door opened, and the eldest, Aster, appeared, carrying a cup of wine. She handed it to Val. "We always share a cup with guests, for friendship's sake. My father forgot to tell us your name."

"My name is Val. Thank you for the wine." He pretended to take a sip while he wondered blankly how to pretend to finish the cup under her watchful eyes.

"A proper name for a prince."

"I suppose it is, but I am a soldier, returning home after battle."

Her brows rose. "And you stopped here, to try for a crown on your way. You should have kept going. There is nothing for you here but what you escaped in battle."

Patricia A. McKillip

He smiled, holding her eyes, while he poured the wine into a boot standing at his knee. "There are better memories here," he said, and tilted the cup against his mouth as if he were draining it dry.

He stretched out on the bed when Aster left, and did not move when he heard the door open again. "Look at him," one of them mocked. "Sleeping as if he were already dead."

"I put a stronger potion into the wine," another answered. "His eyes were far too clear."

Then he heard laughter in the princess' bedchamber, and the sound of cupboards, chests, and cases being opened. He waited, watching them while he pretended to snore. They dressed themselves in bright silks, and lace and creamy velvet gowns; they tied the ribbons of new satin dancing slippers around their ankles. They took rings and earrings and strands of pearls out of their jewel cases, and they spun one another's hair into amazing confections threaded with ribbons. Val had thought them beautiful before; now they seemed enchanted, exquisite, unreal, as if he had drunk the wine and were dreaming them. He was so entranced, he forgot to snore. Aster came to look sharply at him through the open door, but another sister only laughed.

"He sleeps so deeply, he has forgotten how to breathe."

Aster went to a bed in the middle of the chamber. She knocked three times on the carved headboard, and the entire bed abruptly disappeared, leaving a dark, oblong hole in the floor. Like a grave, Val thought, feeling his heart beat at the strangeness of it. In a long, graceful line, beginning with A and ending with M, the princesses descended into the earth.

The wet pool of wine at the bottom of one boot cleared Val's amazed thoughts a little as he pulled them on; he remembered to fling his worn cloak over his shoulders before he left. He glanced into one of the many mirrors in the bedchamber as he hurried after Mignonette. *There is no soldier,* the mirror told him. *The room is empty.*

Fearing that the hole in the earth might close behind the princesses, he followed too closely. His first step down the broad, winding steps caught the hem of Mignonette's gown.

She said, startled, "Who is there? Aster, Lily, someone pulled at my dress."

All their faces looked back toward Val, a lovely, silent chain of princesses stretching down the steps. Aster turned away first, picking up her own silks. "Don't be a goose, Mignonette; you caught your skirt on a splinter."

"The steps are marble," Mignonette muttered. "And I have a bad feeling about tonight."

But no one answered her. Val saw a shining ahead, like a thousand touches of starlight. When they reached the bottom of the stairs, the princesses began to walk down a wide road lined with trees. The leaves on the

Patricia A. McKillip

trees were moonlight, it seemed to Val; they were silver fire. They were silver, he realized finally, with such wonder that he could scarcely breathe. He reached up to touch such beauty, and then, beginning to think again, he broke off a twig bearing four or five leaves to show to the king.

The tree gave a splintering crack as if a branch had fallen; Mignonette whirled again. "What is that noise?" she cried. "You all must have heard it!"

Val held his breath. Her sisters glanced indifferently around them. "It was the wind," one said. "It was fireworks from the dance," another offered.

"It sounded," Aster said lightly, "like a heart breaking."

They turned then onto another broad, tree-lined road. Val closed his eyes and opened them again, but what he saw did not change: All the leaves on these trees were made of gold. Like tears of gold they glowed and shimmered and melted down the branches; they flowed into Val's outstretched hand. Again he broke the slenderest of twigs; again the tree made a sound as if it had been split by lightning.

"Another broken heart," Aster said after Mignonette had screamed and complained, and her sisters had bade her to stop fussing so, they would never get to the dance. Only Val heard her whisper, as she trudged after them, "I have a bad feeling about tonight."

On the third road he broke off a cluster of leaves

made of diamonds. They burned of white fire in the moonlight, a light so pure and cold, it hurt his eyes. Mignonette stamped her foot and wailed at the sound the tree made, but her sisters, impatient now, only hurried toward the lake at the end of the road. Only Aster slowed to walk with her. Her voice was as calm as ever as she spoke to Mignonette, but she searched the diamond-studded dark behind them now and then, as if she sensed their invisible follower.

"I have a bad feeling about tonight," Mignonette said stubbornly.

Aster only answered, "We are almost there. One more night and we will never have to leave again."

On the shore of the lake, twelve boats waited for them. Out of each boat rose a shadowy figure to take the hand of the princess who came to him and help her into the boat. Val paused almost too long, trying to see the faces of the richly dressed men who were pushing the boats into the water. He whispered, suddenly sick at heart, "I have a bad feeling about tonight."

He realized then that the boats were floating away from him. He stepped hastily into the last one; it rocked a little until he caught his balance. Mignonette, whose boat he had the misfortune to enter, promptly raised her voice, calling to her sisters, "I think someone got into the boat with me!"

Her sisters' laughter fell as airily as windblown petals around them; even the man who rowed her smiled.

Patricia A. McKillip

"Don't fret, my Mignonette. I could row a dozen invisible guests across the water." His mouth did not move, Val saw, when he spoke. His eyes were closed. And yet he rowed steadily and straight toward the brightly lit castle on the other side of the lake. Torches burned on all its towers and walls; its casements opened wide; candlelight and music spilled from them. Val, his heart hammering, his hands as cold as if he waited for the beginning of a battle, did not dare move until Mignonette left the boat. The man, pulling it ashore, commented puzzledly, "It does seem heavier than usual."

"You see!" Mignonette began. But he only put his arm around her as she stepped ashore, and kissed her with his mouth that never moved.

"Never mind, my smallest love," he said. "Tomorrow you will have nothing to fear ever again."

Val, following them into the castle, saw the light from the torches at the gate fall over their faces. He stopped abruptly, his bones turned to iron, and his blood turned to ice at what he saw. "This," he heard himself whisper, "is the worst thing that could be."

Still, he forced himself into the castle, to watch the dance.

In the vast hall where the music played, the walls glowed with rare, polished wood. Traceries of gold leaf outlined the carvings on the ceiling. Candles in gold and silver and diamond holders stood everywhere, illumining the princesses' enchanting, sparkling faces. They began to dance at once, smiling into the faces of their princes, who may once have been handsome but who, to Val's unenchanted eyes, had been dead a day too long. Their lips were grim, motionless gashes in their bloodless faces; their eyes never opened. The room was crowded with watchers, all holding empty wine cups and tapping a foot to the music. The music, fierce and merciless, never let the dancers rest; it sent them breathless and spinning around the floor. Ribbons came undone, hems tore, pearls broke and scattered everywhere. Still, the princesses danced, their smiles never wavering at the faces of the dead who danced with them. Their satin slippers grew soiled and scuffed; the thin fabric wore through, until their bare feet blistered against the gleaming floor. Still, they danced, driven by blind musicians who had no reason to rest; they had left their lives elsewhere.

"What a celebration there will be tomorrow night!" Val heard many times as he waited. "The wedding of twelve princesses, and a dance that will never end!"

As the lake grew gray with dawn, the music finally stopped. In silence, drooping with exhaustion in their boats, the princesses were returned to the far shore, where they kissed the frozen faces of their princes and bade them farewell until tomorrow. Val walked ahead of them this time so that he could reach his bed and pretend to sleep before they came back. He kept pace with Aster. She looked a wilted flower, he thought; her eyes seemed

Patricia A. McKillip

troubled, now, but by what she could not imagine. She stumbled a little, on pebbles or the bright, sharp metal of fallen leaves, wincing where her shoes had worn through to her bare feet. He wanted to take her hand, help her walk, comfort her, but he guessed that, in such a place, he could be less alive to her than the dead.

When he saw the stairs, he paused to take off his boots so that he could run up without being heard. As he passed Aster, a boot tilted in his hand, spilling a little red wine on the steps. He saw Aster's eyes widen at it, her step falter. But she did not speak to her sisters. Nor did she say anything when, moments later, she found him sleeping in his bed. Another sister said tiredly, "At least he'll die before we wake. And then no one will have to die for us again."

He waited until they were all hidden in their beds, and nothing moved in the room but morning light. Then he rose, and crept out, with his boots in one hand and the magical leaves in the other, to speak to the king.

The king was pacing outside his daughters' bedchamber; he had not slept that night, either. His hand tightening and loosening and tightening again on his great sword, he gazed wordlessly at Val out of his lightless eyes until Val spoke.

"They go down to the underworld," Val said. "They dance with the dead." He showed the king the three sprays of leaves, silver, gold and diamond, that could only have come from such an enchanted place. His hand trembled with weariness and horror; so did his voice.

"Tomorrow night, they will wed their dead princes, and you will never see them again."

The king, with a shout of rage and grief, tore the leaves from Val's hand and flung open the bedchamber doors. Exhausted, astonished faces appeared from between the hangings in every bed. The king showed them the leaves; sunlight flared from them, turned gold and silver and diamond into fire. "What are these?" he demanded. "Where are they from? You tell me, daughters. Tell me where to go get them. And then I will know where to go to find you."

They stared at the leaves. Little by little, as if before they had only dreamed themselves awake, their faces came alive to terror and confusion. From beneath their beds came the sound of a great, splintering crack, as if a tree had been struck by lightning, or a heart had broken.

Mignonette was the first to burst into tears. "No, it isn't real," she sobbed. "It was a dream! You can't have taken those leaves from a dream!"

"Val followed you," the king said while all around him his daughters wept as if their hearts had broken. "He brought these back with him to show me."

"How could it have been real?" Aster whispered, shivering in her bed while tears slipped down her face. "We were—we pledged ourselves in marriage to—we danced with—"

"Dead princes," Val said. She stared at him, her face as white as alabaster. "Which dead princes?" she asked

Patricia A. McKillip

him. "The ones our father killed because of us?"

"I don't know," he answered gently, though he shuddered, too, at the thought.

She closed her eyes against a nightmare. "You might have died, too, Val, if you had not kept watch."

"I knew someone followed us," Mignonette sobbed to her sisters. "I tried to tell you. And you would not believe me!"

"You were all enchanted," Val said.

Aster opened her eyes again, looked at him. "Did I know you were there?" she wondered softly. "Or did I only wish it?"

There was another sound, the clang of the king's great sword as he drew it from the scabbard and flung it to the floor. Then he took the crown from his head and held it out to Val. "Take my kingdom," he said with great relief. "You have broken the spell over my house, and over me. I no longer want to rule; there are too many innocent dead among my memories."

"Well," Val said uncertainly, turning the crown, which looked too big for him, over in his hands. "There are worse things that could be."

He lifted his eyes, looked at Aster, for comfort, and for friendship. She smiled a little, through her tears, and he saw that she agreed with him: There were worse things that could be than what he had: a kingdom and a choice of flowers from A to M.

Patricia A. McKillip writes: "I read all kinds of fairytales when I was young. I loved the eerie and wonderful illustrations by Fritz Kredel in the copy of *Grimms' Fairytales* my parents gave me. They made the tales seem from a different world, strange and frightening and comical, where donkeys talked and parents tried to kill their children, where love turned into terror, and terror into a life lived 'happily ever after.'

"I chose to retell 'The Twelve Dancing Princesses' because it has elements that stirred my imagination: an unlikely hero, twelve troublesome princesses instead of one; a subterranean world, which might be the place where dreams begin, or maybe where they end. It all depends on how you tell the story."

McKillip is the author of many magical books for children and adults, and has won both the World Fantasy Award and the Mythopoeic Award. Her novels include *Riddle-Master: The Complete Trilogy*, *The Sorceress and the Cygnet*, *The Moon and the Face*, and *Song for the Basilisk*.

She lives in the Catskill Mountains of upper New York state.